THE ANASAZI

AND

THE VIKING

A. TANNER SMITH

Sunstone Press
Santa Fe, New Mexico

Illustration and cover design by Janice St. Marie.

First Edition
Author: A. Tanner Smith
Printed in the United States of America

Library of Congress Cataloging in Publication Data:
Smith, A. Tanner, 1910-
     Anasazi and the Viking / A. Tanner Smith.--1st ed.
        p. cm.
     ISBN: 0-86534-152-4 : $10.95
     1. Pueblo Indians--Fiction. 2. Indians of North America--First
     contact with Occidental civilization--Fiction. 3. America-Discovery
     and exploration--Norse--Fiction. I. Title.
     PS3569.M442A53   1991
     813' .54--dc20   91-4039
                       CIP

Published in 1992 by SUNSTONE PRESS
Post Office Box 2321
Santa Fe, NM 87504-2321 / USA

IN MEMORY OF
My wonderful wife
"My Bobbie"
who loved reading, bridge,
the Rocky Mountains
and
all her children
- and me.

*Cliff dwelling
at Mesa Verde*

Spruce Tree House

PREFACE

Perhaps it is asking too much of the reader to accept a story in which a Viking warrior wanders into a settlement of Anasazi Indians in southwestern Colorado over 800 years ago. But it could have happened. The likelihood of Vikings being present on the Atlantic coastline at the time the Anasazi ("The Ancient Ones") Indians were living at Mesa Verde (now one of the largest and most well preserved pre-historic sites in the United States) is a valid consideration. Archaeologists have dated the occupation of Mesa Verde as 1100 to 1300 A.D. and some have placed the first Viking settlement in America at about 1100 A.D. or later.

Although the Mesa Verde archaeologists have a fairly good basis for their dates, the dates of Vikings in America are more uncertain. But they could have paralled the Mesa Verde dates according to Johannes Brondsted in his book, *The Viking,* in which he states:

"To my mind, there is no reason whatsoever to doubt that the Norse colonists of Greenland did find America at the close of the Viking period (around 1100 A.D.) or in later Middle Ages (1100 to 1400 A.D.) and did endeavor to establish a permanent foothold there - but where a population was apparently hostile."

The meeting of the two cultures in this story could have happened long before Columbus discovered America. The customs and routines of life, both in Mesa Verde and in Norway, are factually based on materials gathered from the Museum at Spruce Tree House, on Mesa Verde, in Colorado; from *America Indians in Colorado* by J. Donald Hughes; from *The Vikings* by Johannes Brondsted; from *Story of Mesa Verde* by Gilbert R. Wenger; from *Ancient Cities of the Southwest* by Buddy Mays and Joseph C. Rumberg, Jr.; from *Compton's Encyclopedia;* from *Down the Colorado* the diary of John Wesley Powell; from *Grand Canyon (An Anthology),* by Bruce Babbitt; and from "National Geographic", March / 1970.

All locations mentioned in this novel, other than the "Valley of the Tall Ones" and the place of the "Devil Bird," actually existed some 800 years ago - and the locations still exist for visitors to see: Spruce Tree House, Balcony House, and Sun Temple at Mesa Verde; the haunting Canyon de Chelly (Canyon de Shay) in Arizona; the Indian town of Supai in the Grand Canyon (known as the Indians' "Shangri-La"); the mountain town of Ouray (called the "Switzerland of America"); and part of the Rocky Mountains near Durango, Colorado.

Conversations and expressions in the Anasazi language are obviously impossible in this story, since it is set 800 years ago.

I hope the reader enjoys the meeting of these two cultures as much as I have enjoyed placing them together.

A. Tanner Smith
September/1991

CHAPTER 1

I t was dusk and Thorvar was hungry. He had traveled far on foot that day and he was tired after climbing up the high Mesa. He found a group of tall, stalky weeds, nearly as tall as himself with extremely large, long seeds pods. There were silky strings like hair hanging from them. He stripped off one of the large leaves covering a pod and saw what looked like rows of yellow, red, and black teeth-like kernels.

As he sank his teeth into this unlikely food, he heard a low snarling sound and looked up to see a large cat-like animal crouching with bobbed tail sticking straight out. Instinctively, Thorvar quickly backed up. Suddenly his feet slipped out from under him and he fell backwards. He tried to grab some weeds to break his fall, but rapidly slipped downward on a slick rock surface. He fell into space, too late aware that he had backed off the edge of a cliff. He felt severe pain from his large body crashing onto some solid object below seconds before he blacked out.

Some time later he recovered consciousness and as he slowly opened his eyes saw many half-clothed people crowded around him. Sensing danger from these people, who resembled some cruel Indians he encountered months before, he started to jump up and attempt to escape. But he suddenly realized he couldn't move his legs - they were numb. His Viking fury and fighting spirit forced him to try again, and although he strained to rise, he couldn't. At that moment as terrible pain enveloped his head and back, he fell back into unconsciousness.

As he slowly regained consciousness and opened his eyes he now saw nothing but darkness. As his eyes became accustomed to the dark, he realized he was in some sort of cave with high ceiling. He lay back in pain and felt someone putting mud or some kind of wet pulp on his forehead. This movement was gentle, but he felt trapped and tried to escape. Once again, his legs failed him. He could only lie back, suffering from the sharp pains. Frustrated, he reached up and grabbed what had been placed on his forehead and angrily threw it away.

Soon, hands replaced this pack in a gentle but firm manner and he heard the quiet voice say, "Na Na." He pushed the person aside, tried to rise and again fell into unconsciousness. The gentle person stayed by him until sunrise. When the "hurt one" began to breathe evenly and deeply she quietly slipped away.

Thorvar was awakened by a strange noise close by sounding like "turk-turk" mixed with "gobble-gobble." He sat up and saw many large birds penned in against the back wall where the ceiling was lower. They were similar to the wild turkeys he had seen near the Viking Colony back east in this expansive land, where he and his comrades had settled by the shores of the great Atlantic Ocean. It was there that he and two close comrades were captured a year ago, when the people in their village were surprised and besieged by fierce Indians. He winced when he recalled how many of his fellow Norsemen and their families had been slaughtered before the Indians were driven off.

It seemed like a long time ago when he and one hundred and sixty men and women made the perilous trip in three Viking ships from Norway across the Atlantic, by way of Greenland, to this new land. They had helped their fierce leader, Thorfinn Karlsefni, settle a colony on those wild eastern shores. This was the land that one of their great explorers, Lief Ericson, had discovered and named "Vinland" (Vineland) because of the wild grape vines and wheat they had found there.

Suddenly his thoughts were interrupted by three small men. One was old and stooped. Thorvar tried to stand, but his legs didn't respond, so he lay there as they cautiously approached him. The old man and one of the younger ones bent over him examining his forehead as he stared defiantly back. The older man pushed the point of a sharp stone hard against his left leg. Thorvar barely felt it but this action by the old man irked him and he pushed him away.

The three men huddled off to the side, apparently talking to each other - and then left, easing their way through a crowd of short, scantly clothed men, women and children, who had gathered to watch.

He looked at all these brown-skinned black-haired people, wondering where they had come from. He looked around and, in amazement, saw structures built of layers of rock, some built as square rooms, some as round towers, and some as tall square buildings with one room apparently built on top of the other. All of these were built within this large cave with a wide open front located high up in a cliff (Spruce Tree House -Mesa Verde.) What sort of people and countryside had he wandered into?

For many weeks he had walked each day toward the setting sun, after finally escaping from nomad Indians camping in the mountains. The mountains were the highest and rockiest he had seen in his year of endless journey, twice as a captive, through this immense, empty land. The many deep and rocky canyons of those mountains reminded him of the deep, sheer gorges of his homeland in Norway. He had followed several rushing streams out of those mountains. Then he had traveled for a week through more arid, sandy countryside with scrubby bushes and weeds.

Now he lay in this large cave, high on a cliff, with strangely quiet people who lived in homes built of layers of rock. He noted that these rocks had been placed in walls in a way similar to the ones he had seen in castles back in England, when, as a young boy, he had gone on raids in that country with his father, his uncle, and their Viking comrades.

As he looked around, he noticed a slim young woman talking to those gathered near him. They then slowly turned and walked away. That is, all except two small boys, who ran over by him. Each grabbed a rock and pushed them against his left leg. He realized they were merely mimicking what their elders had done earlier. However, the older boy then threw his rock hard, hitting Thorvar in the chest. Almost instantly, the young woman rushed over saying. "Na Na!" She took him by the arm and they disappeared.

Shortly afterwards she reappeared carrying a gray pottery bowl filled with what looked like mud mixed with crumpled leaves. She quietly but firmly placed some of this "mix" on his forehead over his injury, smiled and said, "Na Na." Then she gently took hold of the lower part of his right leg and started pushing upward on it trying to make it bend. He realized she was trying to get movement into the leg so he tried hard to bend the knee. With her help he did manage to bend it a little. Then she repeated with the left leg, but in spite of his effort to assist, he could not bend it at all.

She frowned and left but soon returned with mushy food in a pottery bowl and two large pieces of what looked like turkey legs and another bowl filled with water. He was very hungry and now for the first time, smiled at her, nodded thanks, and ripped the meat from the bones. She sat quietly until he was finished. He pointed to himself and said, "Thorvar." She pointed at him: "Toe-war?" Then.... pointed gracefully to herself and whispered, "Ne No."

Later that afternoon, two men and this same woman came carrying some small branches and leaves. She made a bed for him on the floor of the cave and then placed a woven mat over them. The two men gently lifted him onto this makeshift bed. As darkness settled, most of the natives retired to their rock-walled homes high up in the cliff.

Thorvar realized that he was being treated kindly by these primitive people, whom he didn't know, and who certainly must be puzzled by this large, muscular stranger with the light colored skin, blue eyes, and blond hair. He thought to himself, "My appearance is much different from theirs. They do not know me. Why, why would they be so kind to me? I have lived where most people have been brash and inconsiderate of each other, except within their own families. Our people have been cruel to inhabitants in our Viking raids in other countries. Why are these people so different? There must be a hidden reason. I'd best be on my guard."

Slowly he drifted off to sleep.

CHAPTER 2

T hings were much the same for several weeks.

Ne No flexed each of his legs daily and cared for all his needs. The older man came with her on several occasions and each time he gently poked Thorvar's legs with the sharp pointed stone. He felt the prodding more each time. The old man would nod his head in approval and then do a slow dance while mumbling a sing-song chant as he spinkled a handful of crumpled leaves on the Viking's legs. Ne No bent his legs a little farther each day and he accepted these ritual.

After several more weeks, one of the younger men and Ne No were able to get him up on his feet and he took steps slowly, although his left leg continued to drag along somewhat.

The inhabitants generally shied away from him (except for occasional side glances from some of the younger women, some curious children, and a number of sniffing dogs). Thorvar noticed this but decided it was because the men and most of the women were unsure of him with his larger size and different appearance. Further, most of the men seemed to have much work to do above the cave, since they climbed up the side of the cliff wall each morning.

Others were out most of the day hunting for food. When the men returned late in the day, many went down ladders into various large, round covered holes beneath the cave floor. Thorvar wonder why.

He also noticed that some of the women were busy carrying water in large pottery bowls on top of their heads. Others were gathering wood for fires from the canyon below. Most of the rest of them kept busy weaving baskets or molding pottery bowls of clay, which they then baked in the hot ashes of their fires. Afterwards, they painted designs on them in black and red colors obtained from several different kinds of earth and plants. The remainder were busy weaving mats and sandals and preparing food. The children ran and climbed everywhere, some even climbed over him.

Although he was generally ignored, he noticed one man who seemed to be doing nothing most of the time but watching from a distance whenever Ne No came to bring him food and exercise his legs. He thought little of it. However, one night after he had fallen asleep and slept soundly for many hours, he was suddenly aroused by a movement near him. He heard a rattling sound close by. He opened his eyes and saw, in the early morning light, not more than three feet from his head, a large snake coiled with its triangular head raised and facing him, ready to strike. He lay very still and tried to breathe shallowly and not blink his-eyelids.

Even though it was in the cool of the morning, sweat formed on his brow dribbled down into his eyes, causing them to sting. The snake continued to glare, constantly sticking out its forked tongue and then, after a long time, dropped its ugly head and wiggled away. Thorvar sat up and wiped the sweat from his face and eyes. He found himself embarrassed and angry because for one of the few times in his life, he was not able to fight back.

Several nights later, shortly before sunrise, he awakened with a feeling that someone was nearby. As he opened his eyes, he saw the silhouette of a human arm raised overhead holding a large object, which suddenly and powerfully descended toward his head. Thorvar instinctively rolled into the feet of the attacker as the large rock crashed to the cave floor, grazing the top of his head.

He grabbed the person's legs, pulling him down on himself and seized him in a vicious bear-hug. The attacker tried to gouge his eyes out as Thorvar roared, "So you want to get rough." With that outburst he began banging his adversary's head against the cave floor. But the other seized his throat in both hands. In desperation he began strangling Thorvar in a vice-like grip.

The Viking, now desperate for breath, called upon his great strength to rise up and stand on his one good leg, with his enemy still hanging onto his neck. Thorvar then began pounding both fists into the face of his antagonist until he finally relinguished his hold. Then Thorvar threw him to the cave floor, fell on him, grabbed the large rock which had been thrown at his head, and was about to slam it into the other's head, when he was seized by three men who managed to wrestle the rock away from him. Two more rushed up, subdued his attacker and took him away.

Thorvar later learned that their fight had aroused many of the cliff dwellers from their sleep and that this man was not a member of their clan. He had come from another settlement some distance away, up an adjoining canyon where there was a shortage of women. He was the man who had been watching for days as Ne No exercised his legs and brought him food. This stranger had come to take her home as his mate, and when he saw her paying so much attention to Thorvar, he became jealous. After this attempt and his confession that he placed the snake near Thorvar earlier, the Indian was told by the Council never to come back again or he would be thrown from their highest cliff. These facts Thorvar did not know at the time and so reminded himself, once again, to be on guard at night.

Ne No did not know how to explain this to him so she decided it was time for them to learn to talk to each other. It was a slow process, but over a period of several months Thorvar began to learn their language, first by signs and then by words.

Many times during his recuperation Thorvar became impatient to get on with finding his way to another "ocean of water," which he thought must be nearby. "Surely," he thought, "after a year of traveling toward the setting sun, I must be near some ocean." He yearned to sail again on those great waters, but winter was approaching and he realized, after the harsh winter he had endured in those high rocky mountains many months ago, that he could not survive such a trip with only one good leg if he should encounter more such mountains.

As the leaves began to turn shades of orange and brown intermingled with brilliant touches of yellow and red, crowned by a sky of deep azure blue with clouds drifting overhead, the solitary Norseman resigned himself to the fact that he would have to spend the winter with these cliff people.

While he sat there enjoying this thought, he relaxed and looked around at the many things he had not really seen until now.

He noticed the women, mostly short and thin - about five feet tall - busily doing their daily chores. Some were sitting on the cave floor rubbing round stones back and forth across shallow bowl-shaped slabs of rock, grinding kernels into course particles. Ne No had told him this was maize, which they grew in fields above their cliffs.

One thing that puzzled him was the unusual shape of the childrens' heads. Most were flat across the back. He also noticed that the infants, lying beside their mothers, were secured in rigid cradleboards with no padding for their heads. Ne No happened along and he asked her about this. She said it was the custom for mothers to carry their babies on cradleboards on their backs while helping in the fields. Being tied to the hard cradleboards protected the babies' necks.

He noticed other women cooking over large open fires on the cave floor. Bread was baking on thin slab of stone resting on a part of the large fires. Meat was being stewed in large earthen pots and one of the women was crumpling up leaves from wild plants (mustard, saltbush, and wild onions) for flavoring. Meat was broiled over one open fire and another large pot had beans in simmering water.

He limped over to another part of the cave where women were weaving strands of yucca plants and turkey feathers into mats. When Thorvar asked what they would use them for, one explained, "To wrap around us when it is very cold and to sleep on."

He asked, "Is this why you keep so many turkeys penned up?"

"Yes, but sometimes we eat them when the hunters find nothing."

"Do you use their parts for other things?"

"We use the big bones for digging and other things and the small bones for sewing and weaving."

During the night a cold wind blew up through the canyon and the next morning it was still cold. Thorvar noticed that many of the cliff dwellers, who had been wearing very little other than loin cloth and sandals during the long period of warm weather, had now put on sleeveless animal skins. Others were wearing what looked like cotton shirts plus the usual loin cover. Some of them were now wearing their sandals stuffed with soft bark, corn husks or feathers. Over in one end of the cave he saw many of the men carrying large pieces of pink sandstone, from the canyon below, up the path that came from the spring. They carried these rocks to where other men were working beside a dwelling on the other side of the cave.

Thorvar saw some men sitting on the floor using hard, white stones to shape large blocks of soft granular sandstone into blocks that formed the walls of a dwelling. He also noticed that after they were roughly shaped to a general size, they were passed along to others who were building walls of a new added room using mud as a mortar.

After a time, he walked over, sat down beside them, and picked up a hand-sized, hard white stone. One of the men reached over and grabbed the stone away from him. Thorvar, in turn, jerked the stone back and started rubbing and hammering on a large unshaped block of sandstone.

His adversary started to interrupt, then hesitated, watching what this white skinned man was doing. Then he began to smile and called to the other workmen to look. They began laughing and talking loudly. Then several came over, patted Thorvar on the back and sat down beside him to show him how to shape his irregular pink rock.

They gave him one of their small hand mauls. It was made of a stone with a wooden handle, bound together by a leather strip. They showed him how to knock off the larger irregular bumps before using his newly acquired tool to rub the stone into the proper shape for building a wall. He continued working with them the rest of the day and thus became accepted into their community.

And so it was that Thorvar spent the winter with the cave people high up on the side of a cliff.

In the course of the fairly mild winter, he mated with Ne No and went to live with her parents as was their custom.

CHAPTER 3

When spring came, Thorvar still could not travel great distances, although his left leg was almost normal.

Ne No was now pregnant and this influenced him to stay although his spirit of adventure urged him to explore.

He was now able to communicate in words and with sign language, not only with Ne No but with others as well, so he no longer felt left out. They began asking him questions about who he was since his skin, hair, and eyes were so unlike any they had seen. They were also curious about his height. He was a head taller then any of them, he was heavier, and he had broad muscular shoulders. They liked him because he was friendly and they wanted to know most of all where he came from.

One evening, sitting around a large fire, he told them about his journey. He recounted the voyage with one hundred and sixty countrymen, including some women and children. They had sailed across a large ocean in three ships from his faraway home in Norway. He told how it took several months to make this dangerous trip before disembarking on the shores of this land. There they had built their homes as a Viking colony by the shores of the rising sun.

He told them how, a year and a half later, fierce Indians raided their settlement, killing many of their people. He and two of his comrades were captured, although they had fought fiercely and had killed many of their enemies.

When captured, they were forced to go with these Indians, traveling mostly by foot, but occasionally by river, for a period of several months toward the setting sun. Thorvar told of how, while they were camped in an area with many hills and trees, they saw a place where three rivers joined - two smaller rivers into a larger one. They realized that the large river (the Ohio) would be flowing toward an ocean.

One dark night they managed to escape in one of the canoes and paddled with all their strength down the large river. They were pursued, but outdistanced the Indians over a period of several days and nights.

At this point, Thorvar stood up, stretched, and told them there was more to tell, but it was getting late and he would finish another night. They protested, saying they wanted to hear more now.

So he continued relating how for many weeks they traveled down this river until one day they entered into an even larger one flowing southward (the Mississippi). They paddled with much effort across this swift wide river, and finally got to the far side and made camp.

That night they were attacked by another large group of Indians and although they fought fiercely, his two comrades were killed and he was taken captive. He related how these nomad Indians headed west for a great many days until they arrived at the "Shining Mountains" (Colorado Rocky Mountains) where he escaped. After many hardships traveling alone and on foot, he had fallen from the top of their cliff one evening when surprised in the dusk by a cat-like animal. The cliff dellers were fascinated by his story but questioned its truth since they had never heard of such a great distance of so many river, or of any "ocean."

The only thing they had heard of and a few of them had seen were the high shining mountains. "But," they said, "the sun rises over these mountains, not over some great body of water as he said."

The next evening they asked him to tell them about his great country, which he said was far across the water. Thorvar declined but said he would tell them some other time.

Several weeks went by before they again asked him to tell of the strange land far across the water. He said it was too late, since the sun was already going down and he would have much to tell. But if they would gather tomorrow, he would do as they asked.

The next day, late in the afternoon, all the people and some other families living a little distance away gathered together, since the word had gotten around that this large, light-skinned mate of Ne No's was a "great story teller with a great imagination."

Thorvar arose and was about to start talking when one of those near the back, who apparently was seeing Thorvar for the first time, loudly asked, "What have you done to your skin and hair to make them so much lighter than ours and so ugly?"

Thorvar called back, "I have not done anything. This is the way I was born. Most of the people in the country from where I came have light colored skin and hair.

The same person replied, "I have heard that you came across a large body of water in something you called a boat. Where did you find these boats?"

Thorvar replied, "We made them out of strong wood from large trees we cut down."

This unusually belligerent and loud-mouthed Indian said, with a sneer in his voice, "You talk with big mouth, strange one, and tell many things that are not so."

This caused many of those gathered to become upset. and one man, much larger than most of the other men, rose and called to the belligerent one, "You, Ratum, are not welcome here. You are the one with the big mouth and you are mean. This is why we made you leave us four moons ago and told you to go live in another cave away from us. You are still not welcome here. Say no more or we will make a prisoner of you and throw you off our highest cliff."

Ratum did not reply and they all began to settle down to hear the story teller speak. The sun was getting lower in the sky and was shining into the open front of the cliff dwelling. Thorvar stood in this opening so the sun would not be in his eyes as he talked to them. He wanted to be able to see their reactions.

He began by telling them of his own country, of its beauty, its forested hills and snow-draped mountains much like their Shining Mountains. In his country there were many more mountains although they were not as high. He described how water completely filled many of the narrow but deep fjords and told them about the sea.

He told of the rain and snow in the winter and said that some parts of his country was like this past winter he had spent with them in their cliff dwellings. Other parts of his country were very cold, so cold that in part of the country, which had small inland bodies of water, it would freeze the top of the water so solid that they could walk across the surface without fear of falling in.

At this point, one of the more bold men said, "You are telling us that you could walk on the water without falling in and getting wet?"

"Yes, Do you remember how this past winter there were cold mornings when we would arise and notice that water which we had left in our bowls overnight had shiny thin covering?"

When the man nodded his head in agreement, Thorvar continued "Well, that's how some of our inland bodies of water became so thick with ice that not only can people walk on the lakes, but they could stand the weight of men riding on horses."

"What do you mean by men riding on horses? What is a horse?"

So Thorvar explained about the large, four-legged animals that they tamed and rode, especially when warring against other people.

Suddenly, from far back in the cave came loud laughter. "See what I mean about the lies this strange one tells? Now he says he can walk on water and ride on the back of wild animals." He sneared once more and then ran down a path and disappeared into the canyon below. Just as everyone was quieting down again and Thorvar was preparing to resume his story, suddenly a great shadow filled part of the cave as the sun was blocked out momentarily by some large object flying overhead. Immediately, those present hurriedly carried or dragged their smaller children into their homes. Many of the men, visibly affected by this sudden intrusion, hurried down the ladders into their large, sunken rooms, their kivas, into which they so often withdrew. The visitors cowered in the back of the cave. As Thorvar turned to look at the sky, he felt his right arm gripped by the large Indian, Nakota, who said, "There it goes, see it?"

Thorvar looked where Nakota pointed, and he saw a great bird with a large wingspread rapidly disappearing into the distance. "This is the largest bird I have ever seen, but why is everyone terrified? The bird did no harm and it is flying away."

"You are right, it did no harm this time because we were all gathered here in the cave listening to your stories. But four growing seasons ago while some of our people were tilling the ground above our cliffs where we raise our maize, squash, and sunflower seeds, this bird suddenly swooped down without warning and with its large, clawed feet, grabbed a small boy playing in the fields. We were completely surprised and before anyone could do anything, the bird flew away, carrying Natcha in his claws. We never saw him again.

"Then two growing seasons ago, this devil bird suddenly swooped down again, grabbing in his clawed feet a small girl playing in the fields above. We were able to save her by throwing rocks as the bird tried to rise. It dropped her, hurting her, but she was safe. We have heard stories about the bird from travelers. They have seen it flying near the Shining Mountains and they have been told by others of a large cave in which it lives in those mountains."

Thorvar was deeply impressed and expressed his deep concerned. "Some day when my legs is well and I can travel again, I will go in search of its cave and I will kill that devil bird."

Nakota grabbed him by the shoulders and said, "When you go, I will go with you."

CHAPTER 4

S ome distance north of these cliff dwellings, on the western side of the Shining Mountains, a large tribe of Indians (ancestors of the Apaches) settled in the fall of the year in a beautiful valley pocketed by tall mountains rising on three sides (Ouray, Colorado). This tribe had migrated from the far north looking for warmer country and better hunting grounds. This awesome valley, with its mountain streams and abundant wildlife, seemed a good place to settle. Directly above it was a large shelf of forested land where deer, rabbits, and other game abounded. The people felt protected from surprise attacks, since this valley was enclosed on three sides by steep mountain walls, with only one opening to the north. They felt this necessary because they had attacked numerous smaller tribes in their trek southward, taking food, women, and killing those who stood in their way. They were also moving south because they were a fierce, warring people, who, rather than cultivate crops, preferred to hunt for their food and steal from others who had what they wanted.

This year however, the beautiful fall had been followed by a very cold and harsh winter with heavy snows in the high mountain valley. When the weather finally began to warm, they sent out three tribesmen to scout and determine how they could all get around this mountain and continue on toward warmer weather. As time went by and the scouts did not return, unrest developed among the tribesmen, some wanting to go and others wanting to stay until the scouts returned.

One evening, as the moon reached its fullest, they were surprised to see the moon rapidly covered by heavy clouds. Soon, in the darkness, there were many streaks of brilliant lightning followed by extremely loud claps of thunder.

The thunder seemed to be all around them as it echoed off the mountain sides, rolling progressively from one end all the way around the valley to the other side. The lightning and loud thunder continued all around them until the warriors, became very frightened, saying, "the Mountain Gods are angry with us." Their Chief, also very frightened, said, "Yes, these Mountain Gods are very angry with us. They do not want us here. We will leave in the morning."

During the rest of the night, rain poured down and they could do nothing but stay in their tepees. However, in the morning, with the sun shining brightly, some prepared to leave. Other complained, saying, "What way will we go? We should wait until our three tribesmen return and tell us the way. Otherwise we may wander further into the mountains of the angry Gods." Many others began to agree that they should wait.

They were arguing about this when their Chief called to them for silence - and then pointed to the opening to this valley through which they had originally come. They turned to look and were greatly pleased to see their three tribesmen coming toward them. They surrounded the three, who told them they had found a way, first following small canyons toward the setting sun for some days and then turning toward warmer country.

"As we walked and ran following a mountain stream, the next day we came into flatter, warmer, sandy country where there were small trees and bushes. Several sunrises later, we sighted high cliffs with many caves. There was one cave that was especially large in which men, women, and children lived.

"We quietly circled around these caves some distance away so we would not be seen and then climbed some hills at the back so we could get up on top and look down into the caves, especially the very large one where so many people are living. However, there were men on top, digging around what looked like small weeds - but then we realized they were growing things to eat. So we slipped away and hurried back, running most of the time, during three suns to tell all of you."

Then their Chief asked, "Would we be able to attack them up in their caves?"

And one of them replied, "Yes, it could be done since the men did not look like warriors; further, there should be plenty of food - and women."

The Chief glared at him and said in a loud voice, "I want to know since they are living in caves up in cliffs, will we be able to get up to them?"

The scout replied, "It will not be as easy as in the past, where tepees and places to live dug in the ground were easy to attack. But there is a path they use to climb from the canyon up to the caves. And there are places in the cliff rock sides where we can climb up to them. They do not look like warriors - they are small and weak and have no lookouts. We can surprise and overcome them easily."

However, what these scouts did not know was that since the "Devil Bird" had reappeared, one of the cave people had been hiding each day in the fields above the cave with a bow and arrow, watching for it to return. While he was hidden, Tanoto had seen these three strangers sneaking around, obviously being careful not to be seen by those tending the crops.

As soon as they were gone, Tanoto hurried to the cliff edge and carefully climbed down the side using the toe holes dug in the cliff to descend. He immediately called to some of the men working in the cave. When he told them what he had seen, they all descended the ladder into the largest kiva.

After seating themselves in a circle on the floor, one of the older men said, "Tanoto, why do you think these three are enemies from a warring tribe? They may be friendly and will not even bother us."

Tanoto shook his head, "Why would they be sneaking around looking at all part of our dwellings unless they planned to attack us? If they were friendly, they would have come as other have done, asking for food - and we would have fed them.

"Also, these wore more clothing than we do, which mean they have come from the cold north - and we have heard from others that some tribes from the north are very warlike and cruel - and steal women."

After Tanoto said these things, they all became quite worried and afraid, for they were not warring people and knew very little about how to defend themselves. Some argued that they did not need to worry because they were living up in the cliffs. Others were not so sure. Finally it was agreed by most to have all the men, each evening, do their tribal chant dance to their God spirits, seeking their protection.

So each of the next three evenings this dance was performed to the rapid, rhythmical beat of their chanting. *"Hu*, yu, yu, yu - *Hu*, yu yu yu - *Hu*, yu yu yu - *Hu* yu yu yu."

But Tanoto was not pleased, because no one talked of defending themselves. They were depending entirely on their Spirit Gods to protect them. So he decided to talk to Thorvar, who seemed to be very brave and had told them of how he and other Vikings had fought many battles in his own country. But Tanoto could not find Thorvar. He looked all around and in the back of the cliff dwellings. He climbed ladders to look in various upper floor rooms, sticking his head through narrow doorways into many small rooms.

He finally decided to check in the fields above the cave and walked up several slooping rock ledges which led to the part of the cliff, where the toe holes to the top had been pecked out many years before.

Even though he was in a hurry, he made sure that he started up with his left foot in the bottom hole. He knew that if he started with his right foot, when he reached the half way point, the holes for his foot and his hand had been slanted in such a way that he would suddenly fall all the way into the canyon below. This had also been done as a precaution against an enemy trying to sneak down on them from above.

After looking for Thorvar in the corn fields above, he carefully descended to the cave floor again. Tanoto now began to panic with the thought that Thorvar might have left them to seek out his "Ocean." He decided to check below and hurried down the path into the canyon. As he reached a rather sharp turn in the path almost at the bottom, he glanced to the side, down the dead end canyon. and saw Thorvar. He was relieved to see him, but hesitated to interrupt as he sat quitely talking to Ne No. He had seen them this way many times before and never interrupted. But this time, because of his feeling of urgency, he ran over to where they were obviously enjoying each other's company.

Thorvar seemed quite irked at being interrupted, but when Tanoto told him why, he left Ne No and they walked back up to the dwellings.

Thorvar began to realize the real dangers involved. As he thought of preparing for battle and organizing and fighting a real enemy again, his Viking urge for combat rose in him. With no hesitation, he accepted Tanoto's idea of approaching their Council to see if they would allow Thorvar to prepare them to resist the anticipated attack.

He stood well off to the side while Tanoto argued with several of the older members. Finally, he came over to Thorvar and said that the Council members were all going into their largest kiva to consider this proposal and they wanted both of them there, also. So for the first time, Thorvar climbed down the ladder into the kiva, into the hole in the cave floor he had often wondered so much about.

As he reached the dirt floor of this large round "hole," he saw that the walls, which were about twice the height of the men, were all faced with the same sandstone blocks as the dwellings. Pillars supported the roof and between each pillar were low shelves or benches on which various ceremonial items were placed. The Council members were all seated in the tight circle on the dirt floor, arguing quietly with each other. Since he was not being included, he looked about the kiva and noticed, in the center of the floor, what looked like a firepit. Nakota, seeing Thorvar's interest, slipped over by him and quietly explained how fresh air was drawn in through a hole in the wall shaft. He explained how the fresh air hit a small wall deflector which caused the air to fill the kiva. He showed Thorvar that the smoke from the fire was going out above through the hole that they had entered.

Thorvar whispered, "What is that little hole in the floor over there?"

"That is our Sipapu, from which our Spirits come out of Mother Earth below. It is very important in some of our ceremonies."

A short time later, the Council members called Tanoto and the Viking over to where they were sitting, and asked Thorvar, "Do you agree with Tanoto that there is a danger that we might be attacked by these Indians coming down from the north."

He replied, "From my experience with different Indian tribes in my travels, twice as their captive, I have seen and experienced their cruelty. They are not peaceful and friendly people like you. They kill anyone just to get food and to take women. And they especially scorn and are more brutal with those who appear weak and do not defend themselves. Yes! I agree with Tanoto."

"But if we offer them food when they first appear and do not fight, might they be satisfied and not bother us?"

"No! They will think that you are weak, and no better than women. They will kill many of you and take your women and all the food they can find."

The Council members appeared very upset and gathered on the other side of the kiva. After further discussions among themselves they called to Thorvar and asked, "How can we possibly defend ourselves? We are peaceful people, as you have said. We know nothing of how to fight an enemy."

Another one said, "We live in a large cave in a high cliff with some protection from animals. But an enemy such as this from the north can easily climb into our dwellings, just as we do when gathering food, water and wood."

A third member nervously said, "Yes, we did not build in the cliffs to defend ourselves. All around us in the many other cliff dwellings, the people are almost all peaceful. We built up here mostly to get up in drier surroundings with more protection from the weather. How can we possibly defend ourselves?"

Thorvar replied, "You can but it will take much hard work in preparation, much determination and most of all a strong desire to be brave." The Councilmen withdrew, but shortly afterwards turned back to the large Viking, and one of them said, "You have told us of how you and your people across the water have fought and conquered many enemies. Will you show us how to defend ourselves and conquer this enemy?"

To which Thorvar enthusiastically replied. "Yes, but only if you and all of our people do as I say, and work very hard in this preparation. You and all your people must be very brave and fight to the death, if need be. Only on these terms will I aid you."

Each Councilman, in turn, agreed and vowed to see that his people did also. "Tell us your plan of defense. What can we do to help? What can we tell our people?"

The Viking went over and put his arm around Tanoto's shoulder and said, "I would like for you and Nakota to help me."

CHAPTER 5

W ith the old Viking spirit rising up in him Thorvar said, "Since your dwellings are located in the cliff which looks down into a narrow canyon, only a stone's-throw from the other side, this will aid our defense. As to explaining my plan of defense, this must wait. Here are the thing your people must do: I want two men to go down into the canyon, up the opposite side, and go to that highest cliff peak a short distance away. There is an unobstructed view to the north and toward the setting sun, for a great distance across the flatlands, and far beyond our high mesa. I want them there, starting tomorrow, from before the sun rises each morning until complete darkness each evening.

"These must be the most dependable and the fastest runners and climbers in your village, since they will, while on this highest cliff point, be constantly looking for this northern tribe. As soon as they see them, they are to return to me as quickly as possible to report their sightings."

"From the canyon below, cut six long and strong branches. Then bend each into as much of a circle as possible and secure the ends together. It will help to place them in the stream. When completed and dried in the sun, the circle should be a little more than half the height of a man. Then each of these circled sticks should be covered completely on the front side with a lightweight, turkey feather blanket and then covered again with dried, lightweight animal skin. Finally, another straight branch should be secured to each side across the back as a hand hold.

"Thirty men must make bows, similar to the one you make to go hunting, but twice as long. Make many long arrows with stone heads attached. Use heavier yucca cord or sinew for your bow strings. All other men should have their own bows ready with plenty of stone-tipped arrows, not with the woodtips you use to hunt small food animals.

"Place a great many, very large rocks all along the front edge of your cave floor, wherever there is the slightest possibility that anyone could climb up the steep slopes from the canyon below into this cave. These rocks should be about the size of those built into your dwelling walls, and should be piled in two rows, one behind the other, about four rocks high. Also pile rocks above the trail which comes up from the spring in the canyon. If your people cannot find enough rocks to do this, then take them from the walls of your dwellings. They can be rebuilt later.

"Make sure that in all your dwellings on the second or higher levels, that you have a small window opening facing the canyon. If you do not have such an opening, tear out a little from your wall so you do have a canyon view."

At this moment, several of the Councilmen objected, saying, "Why should we worry having a view of the canyon from these dwelling when you say an enemy is coming?" And they complained. "Our people cannot get these things done - it is too much."

Thorvar replied, "I do not have time to explain now. All these things can be done, will be done, unless you want this enemy to overcome you. Further, there is more which should be done!"

He then continued, "Have the women make readily available their largest pottery bowls. They should have at least one from each dwelling. If they do not have large ones, they should get busy right after we stop talking and make them.

"Make new axes with stone heads twice the size that you usually use and with very strong wooden handles half again the usual size. Twelve of these should be made.

"Make up six closely woven, thick fiber baskets that will fit securely upside-down over a man's head down to this shoulders. When the basket is upside-down over his head, make an opening so he can see out.

"All of this should be started immediately. We may not have more than a few days to prepare."

The Council members who had been sitting quietly in awe of what he was saying, recovered their voices and began saying, almost in unison, "We cannot possible do all this. It is too much for our people to do. We are dommed!"

To which Thorvar replied, "You have a chance to get all of this done by your people if you start now."

One of them implored, "Can we do just some of the more important tasks and forget about the rest?"

Thorvar, wishing to be understanding as well as realistic, considered this request for a time, and then replied. "If you will agree to give Nakota and Tanoto and myself the full authority to instruct your people, with all of you overseeing their work, and place me in complete command of the final arrangements and of the battle with the enemy, I will withdraw two of my eight proposals.

"Make up only two, rather than six, of the thick woven baskets. These were intended to protect your fighers' heads from sharp and heave blows in hand-to-hand combat. Head protection has saved many lives in close combat in my country.

"Forget the one large bowl required of each woman. I had intended these for heating and containing very hot water to be thrown down on the Indian foes who might get up the cliff side. In our country we found that dumping boiling hot water on our enemy caused them to run away scream-ing in pain. They did not come back."

Meanwhile, some days' travel to the north of the cliff dwellings, the Chief had summoned all of the men, following the report of their three scouts, to a parley. After a short time, the Chief, in a very loud voice said, "We will leave now to go to those cliff dwellings where food and women again appear fairly easy to take!!"

Many of the women and children were not so anxious to leave this beautiful, protected valley. The women liked bathing and washing in the cool, clear mountain stream and many of the children enjoyed wading.

The water was so clear that they could see and pick up pretty rocks from the bottom and they enjoyed trying to catch fish with their hands.

During the next few days they all moved and climbed along at a reasonable good pace, since they were well rested from their stay in that beautiful valley. Their larger dogs were able to transport some of the heavier things on animal skins fastened to two long "drag poles." Late the second day, they reached higher ground and were able to look back on the mountains from which they had so recently departed. It was a beautiful view and some of the women cried secretly at having to leave, "because our men can only think of getting where more younger women could be taken for their pleasure and to do their work. Then our men can sit around and do nothing but boast about what great warriors they are for killing men who do not fight." The women whispered to one another that several nights ago, the Mountain Gods seemed to be angry. They had never been angry with them before when the leaves turned different colors, and when the snow fell. And they recalled, there had been many warm days in the sunshine and lots of food. There were many plants that made them well again.

The women further reasoned that maybe the Mountain Gods were not even angry with them, maybe they were angry about something else. One of them sighed as she quietly said, "It doesn't matter what we women think. Our men enjoy hurting weaker braves of other tribes; they enjoy killing them and bragging about it around their campfires."

So the next morning at sunrise, they dutifully arose, got water, prepared food and resumed their long trek. For the next few days they walked through low canyons, following mountain streams. Finally, on the last day, they traveled through flatter and more sandy countryside with many small trees and bushes.

As they made camp on the sixth evening, their braves became quite exited. They had sighted the high mesas in which their scouts said were the caves of the people who could easily be overcome. They boasted of how they would kill those "squaw-like men" and take their women and much food.

The next morning a number of their men, in separate scouting groups, carefully and quietly sneaked up into this higher land to take a closer look at the cliff dwellings. They returned that afternoon to the camp and bragged about how easy it was going to be to surprise them and get into the dwellings from below. Some even said they could attack from above by climbing down using the foot and hand holes these people had pecked in the side of the cliff.

Their Chief then told them that they would leave this very night. Most of them would hide in the canyon just below the cliffs and the rest would go above. After they were all in place they would wait until sunrise, and then, at his signal, all would attack. Coming in from above and below at the same time, they would surprise these unprotected people, kill anyone in their way, and search out and take women and food. He also pointed out four men and told them, "You have proven yourselves to be weak in battle and unfit to be warriors. You will stay with the women and children and at daybreak will lead them toward this higher country. After our victorious battle, we will join you as the sun sets."

And so, during the night, the Chief and his warriors quietly positioned themselves on the canyon floor below the cliff dwellings and at the foot of the path. Another ten were positioned above, ready to climb down the foot and hand holds in the cliff.

CHAPTER 6

A s the darkness became early morning light, the Chief gave his signal. The Indians on the canyon floor began quietly climbing up the steep slope among the small trees and bushes and rocks. At the same time, others were starting their climb up the narrow path.

As they were proceeding stealthily upward, they suddenly heard a great amount of noise above them. Up the slope they saw large rocks bounding rapidly down toward them from all along the cave rim and from above the narrow path. Some found cover but others screamed in agony as these large rocks crashed into them. When it became quiet again, those who had escaped injury, while glancing cautiously upward, carried the injured down into the canyon near their Chief. This unexpected assault bewildered them. After some confusion, their Chief finally said, "Now the big rocks are all gone. Now we'll go up and take them." At the same time, he signaled to his warriors above the cave to start climbing down the cliff.

When the warriors had cautiously crawled about half way up the steep slope, they hid behind large boulders and tree trunks while waiting to see if anything might happen from above. After a time, when all remained quiet, they boldly started up the steep slope yelling their war cry.

However, almost instantly several of them cried out in pain as they clutched at the arrows in their backs. All turned quickly to see where the arrows were coming from and saw many more arrows coming from the other side of the canyon. They heard terrified yells from the dwellers' side and turned just in time to see two of their warriors falling from the face of the cliff. They saw them crash into the canyon below and lie still, just as another cry pierced the air and a third warrior fell to his death.

As they turned instinctively, arrows from the other side of the canyon,were landing all around them. They turned and hid behind large boulders and tree trunks, with their backs to the cliff dwellings, and started shooting their arrows at these new attackers.

Suddenly, the crashing noise began again, as big rocks came tumbling down on them once more from the cliff dwellings. These rocks bounced wildly and pinned several of the attackers against the boulders and tree trunks they had just been using as protection from the arrows. As this wave of rocks passed, they started retreating down the steep slope, still trying to hide from the arrows that were coming from the opposite side of the canyon.

They began running wildly and rolling down the slope in general disarray as more arrows showered down from the windows of the cliff dwellings. Caught in this crossfire, their retreat turned into panic as they all rushed out of the canyon.

When the Anasazi saw the enemy in complete and wild retreat they all cheered and gathered around Thorvar, Nakota, and Tanoto in great excitement. They had fought and defeated a very strong and cruel enemy, with none of them injured and none of them killed.

Three of the Council members after the people quieted down, approached the Viking and the eldest one said, "We shall forever hold you and your name in great respect around our campfires. We will tell our young ones of the great plan you made and how you and Nakota and Tanoto wisely and bravely protected us and our women from this cruel enemy. You will become a part of our legend even though you are of light skin, with your hair like the sun shining on the sandy soil and your eyes the color of the cloudless sky."

Thorvar climbed up on a large boulder, once again with his back to the canyon, facing all of them. In a loud voice he thanked them for these fine words of praise and then said, "It was because you trusted me and Nakota and Tanoto and all of you worked hard and fought as we directed, that you have, at least for the time being, put the enemy to flight.

"However, we must remain alert through the rest of the day and the coming night, keeping all our men with bows and arrows in place in the windows and across the canyon on the other side." Almost immediately, many of the people, including several of the councilmen began protesting, saying they saw no need to continue doing this, and one of the older Councilmen said. "Thorvar, you and all of us saw the enemy fleeing down the canyon, frighted and in disarray. We have beaten them - they will not come back."

Thorvar, still standing on a high boulder, was about to reply when two arrows whistled by, one swishing between his body and his left arm as he raised it sideways in a gesture and the other knicking his right sleeve. He turned quickly to see two Indians below who then disappeared down the canyon.

"Do you still think the enemy has given up?"

The elder Councilman bowed his head and replied, "You are right. We will do as you say."

Meanwhile, the bewildered band of Indians continued their wild retreat, dragging the injured leaving those who appeared to be dead, and falling over rocks and bushes in their flight to escape.

However, two young warriors, Bear Claw and Black Wolf, ashamed of their older warriors' cowardice, stayed and hid behind some rock ledges below the cliff dwellings. While they waited, they heard yells of celebration.

Bear Claw said, "We must kill some of them before we leave so they will also sorrow."

Black Wolf replied, "Yes, but how?" As they kept looking up, trying to think of some revengeful act to show their bravery and cunning, they suddenly saw a large man climb up on a high rock in full view, with his back to them, talking to the cliff dwellers. Black Wolf whispered, "He is so much bigger, he must be their Chief. We will kill him."

Each carefully drew back his bow and released an arrow right at the him as he stood in full view. They were sure both arrows would pierced his body, yet he did not fall but quickly turned around and saw them. They were in utter awe when they saw that he looked like no other person they had ever seen. Bear Claw gasped, "He not only is big but look - his skin is almost as white as the snow and his hair looks so different. He is not like any of us."

Black Wolf whispered, "And our arrows went right through his body and he did not fall. He must be a Mountain God."

They turned and ran just as the older warriors had done. When they finally caught up with the others, who had been slowed down by carrying eight of their wounded, they told their Chief what they had seen.

He replied in a loud voice for all to hear, "We will not fight those who have Mountain Gods among them. That is why I, as your Chief, could not overcome them. We will make well our hurt ones in some sheltered place with our women and children and then go to a warmer place away from these Mountain Gods."

Meanwhile, the Anasazi continued their watch, but next morning, when nothing had occurred, they abandoned their defensive position. The next task was to carry the sandstone blocks from the canyon and replace them in the walls of the buildings. Suddenly, the comparative stillness was shattered by loud screams, as Ne No and several other women came running up the path from the springs below.

One of them said excitedly, "There are two of the enemy Indians lying down, resting on the ground by our spring - and another is lying on a ledge above!"

Ne No added, "Yes, and one of them grabbed my leg and yelled some words at me!"

When Thorvar heard this, he ran over and grabbed one of the shields they had made. He also grabbed one of the long-handled stonehead axes.

Now he was prepared for real Viking combat. Nakota also seized a shield and an axe and followed him.

They hurried quietly down the path, holding their shields in front of them to deflect arrows or a surprise attack. When they were about two-thirds of the way down this path, they left it and began cautiously creeping on down through small trees and shrubs, making certain not to be surprised or ambushed.

As they proceeded, they became concerned since they could not sense any movement by this apparently clever enemy, who had certainly been aroused by the women's screams. Meanwhile, the people crowded up along the outer rim of their dwelling, trying to see what was happening below.

As the Viking and his companion crept further down into the canyon, they suddenly located their enemies, two were still lying by the spring and one was resting on a ledge above. One lifted his arm, apparently gesturing to the one above.

Their apparent fearlessness aroused the ire of both Thorvar and Nakota, and they rose up and with loud war cries, swinging their war axes overhead, bore down on them. The Viking moved to attack the one who had just raised his arm, towering over him with his long stone axe posied over his head, ready to strike. But when the enemies made no effort to protect themselves, they both stopped and stared. It quickly became apparent that the two Nakota was approaching were dead. As the Viking looked back down, the one at his feet gave wild shriek of fear and then relaxed in death.

Thorvar and Nakota sat down on a large rock by the spring to rest for a moment and figure out what had happened. Had someone poisoned the water? Thorvar casually looked up at the blue sky above the sheer wall of the cliffs and as Nakota followed his gaze, both simultaneously began saying to each other, "they are the ones who fell from the climbing holes on the high cliff above."

As they came up the path together, the dwellers began cheering, but they soon quieted down when told of what actually occurred. The Head of the Council then said, "Get these terrible men away from our spring, now. Throw their bodies in the older trash pile that we no longer use."

Thorvar looked around for Ne No to see if she was alright, but could not find her. He was becoming concerned when one of the women who had been with her said, "Ne No has gone in to rest. She was upset by this and her childbirth is not too many full moons away."

He found her in their room and said, "Will you be alright now?"

"Yes, Toe-war. But that bad Indian grabbed me by the leg and tried to pull me down on him as he yelled something at me. And he looked so mean."

So the Norseman sat beside her for a while, feeling her belly, which was beginning to be noticeably larger, and said, "I wonder what he will look like, with you of dark skin, brown eyes, and black hair - and me of light skin, light hair, and blue eyes?"

She smiled at him and replied, "Toe-war, I hope that he looks and acts just like you."

He kissed her and said "You rest now. I am going to help the men carry their building blocks up and replace them in the walls."

He spent most of the rest of the day doing this and by late in the afternoon, they had all done so well in recovering most of the sandstone blocks that were not broken up, that they had to search farther out for those blocks still missing. As he crawled around in the underbrush, he suddenly saw some movement behind a large boulder. His first thought was that it was a wounded Indian hiding, since he couldn't run. He quietly pulled his knife from his belt and with one swift movement jumped around the large boulder, ready to drive his knife into this enemy.

But he pulled up abruntly as he saw, instead of an enemy, the mate of one of the sisters of Ne No. He was sitting on the ground with his knees up against his chest and his head bowed. Beside him lay his bow and arrow, his winter clothing, his pair of heavier sandals, his knife, and his woven sleeping mat.

When Thorvar saw all this he asked, "What are you doing down here in the canyon with all of your possessions?"

He sulked for a while and then finally said, "When I returned my mate, Ne No's sister, had put all of these belongings of mine outside the door to our room. She would not even speak to me and I could no longer enter."

"Oh, don't be so down. If she is mad at you for something, she will soon get over it. It is your home. You have a right to be there. Come, let us go back."

"No. It is no longer my home. She is no longer my mate. I have no rights. I am alone."

That evening, Thorvar told Ne No of what he had seen and heard, and said, "He must be a coward not to come back up and tell her of his rights to be there."

"No, Toe-war. He has no rights to return to their home because, as you say, he is a coward. He ran away and hid while you were all fighting those bad Indians. My sister is ashamed of him and no longer wants to be his mate. When she put all his belongings outside their door, she was telling him that they are no longer mated."

"How can that be, Ne No? It is his home as much as hers."

"No, Toe-war. Where they live belongs to her, just as where my Mother lives belongs to my Mother - and our place belongs to me. This is one of our strongest customs and rights."

"But Ne No, this does not seem right at all. It would not be so in my country. A man then has no place to call his home."

She sat up in bed, put her arms around his neck and quietly said, "Toe-war, do not be so disturbed. He can go back and live in his Mother's home. Anyway, the male mates do not belong to our Mother's Clan, but retain their religious rights with their Mother's Clan, just as you live with us and am my mate but we do not ask you to give up your beliefs and your Mother."

That evening as Thorvar cuddled up against Ne No, he thought to himself how strange and primitive these people were. And yet they had peace among themselves and were content living in such a confined space.

But when he thought of his own year-long confinement here, it made him suddenly restless with the desire to get away to get out into the open spaces. He began thinking about going with Nakota to the Shining Mountains (the San Juan Range, Colorado) to find the cave where the Devil Bird lived.

CHAPTER 7

N akota, who, because of his years of experience in this somewhat arid countryside, had greater knowledge than Thorvar of what to expect in the way of food on their trip to the mountains, told the Viking, "We will not be able, during this hot, dry time of the year, to find much plant or berries. They are more available in the early summer, and we eat nuts and pods in the fall.

"Our most likely meat will be rabbit or rattlesnake. Therefore, we must take from our storage rooms. some of the beans, corn, nuts, and acorns that are left from this past winter."

Thorvar listened attentively since he had been very hungry when he followed those few, small, and almost entirely dry waterways from the Shining Mountains to these cliffs.

Nakota continued, "However, as you know, when we arrive at the mountains, animals and fish will be plentiful."

With foods in small basket packs on each of their backs, long oak bows, a good supply of stone-tipped arrows, hunting knives, freshly made sandals, and some flint stone, they departed early the next morning. They also carried drinking water in small closely woven containers.

Their trip across the arid land was fairly uneventful. By evening they were weary from the heat of the blazing sun and welcomed the cool of the desert after the sun went down. After days of travel, they arrived at the foothills of the mountains.

They wound their way through several valleys in the foothills, following mountain streams for some time, and as the sun began to set behind the higher mountain peaks, Thorvar told Nakota, "Once the sun goes down when you are in the mountains, darkness follows rather quickly. We had better find a place to camp for the night." They found a beautiful spot in a stand of tall silver spruce trees besides a sizeable mountain stream, gathered plenty of fallen wood, and made a campfire for warmth and protection from the wild animals. Then they ate the last of their food, talked for a while, and decided they would take turns keeping the fire going through the night to discourge hungry animals.

As the Norseman lay on the ground between two of the beautiful, tall trees and heard the familiar sounds of the mountain stream bouncing merrily over and around the boulders in its paths, he suddenly felt a wonderful surge of happiness and exuberance at being back in surroundings similar to those of his homeland. And as he lay there with his wonderful memories, he quietly slipped off to sleep to the accompaniment of the soothing and rippling murmurs of the mountain stream.

When Nakota awakened the next morning, he could not find Thorvar anywhere. After some time passed, he thought to himself, "Could it be that this companion of mine has only used the excuse of looking for the Devil Bird, to have me as a guide to get him safely across the barren land to these mountains where he could leave all of us?"

As time passed and he did not return, Nakota became saddened, and began to realize how much he had come to think of Thorvar as his best and most reliable friend. He wondered if he should try to find and kill the Devil Bird himself, or just return to his people after he had rested and found food for his trip home.

As he sat there thinking, he heard something in the bushes on the hillside above him. Suspecting it might be a bear or mountain lion, he quickly place an arrow in his long bow and turned quickly around, ready to launch the arrow as soon as the animal appeared. As he hid behind the trunk of one of the trees, tense and ready, the bushes parted and out strode Thorvar. He did not see Nakota and was taking great strides with a look of happy contentment on his face.

Nakota quickly dropped his bow and rushed toward the Norseman, asking, "Where have you been for so long?"

In great excitement Thorvar said, "I got up at the first glimmer of dawn and climbed up the mountain to where I could see the high peaks with snow on their north sides. It was beautiful and the refreshing smell of pine needles was everywhere. I even saw a deer drinking from a small mountain stream some distance away."

When Nakota told him of his own concerns and doubts when he was gone for so long, Thorvar put his arm around his shoulders and said, "I have come to find and kill that big bird which has caused your people so much sorrow and concern. Above all, I wish to avenge the death of the boy, Natcha, and the little girl who was crippled when she fell from its talons."

He then reached over his shoulder and showed Nakota the squirrels he had killed and said, "Build up the fire - now we will eat some real food."

After they had eaten, the Norseman licked his fingers and said, "I saw several caves above where I was standing. One appeared to be quite large. Shall we go back up where I was and make camp there? Then we could really begin our watch for the Devil Bird, since this is the area where the travelers say they have sighted it."

They filled their water baskets from the mountain stream, picked up the long bows and arrows, secured their hunting knives, and started on up the mountain.

They set up camp by digging into a dirt bank and placing branches with many thick needles as a cover overhead. Then they went hunting for wood and for food.

By evening they had returned from their individual hunts, Thorvar with two ground squirrels and a rabbit - and Nakota with berries, nuts, roots, and some plant leaves. Neither had seen the Devil Bird. They enjoyed a good meal and were soon relaxing around their fire as darkness closed in around them.

Nakota looked over at his companion and said, "All those stories you have told us about the land you came from. Are they true? Or are you just a good story teller with a great imagination, as some of our people have said?"

Thorvar laughed heartily, and then said, "Yes, my friend, everything I have told them is true, not imagined."

"Then you really do ride animals?" asked Nakota in a tone of awe.

"Yes, we use horses for many purposes, especially in battle. They are very strong and run very fast."

"Do your people live in caves as we do?"

"No, but in some rather barren land in our Country other people build rooms of rock and mud mortar as you do - but out in the open, not in cliffs or in caves. In the part of my country where I lived, near where the sun rises, we have large forests of tall trees.

"We cut down the trees and use their trunks, placing one on top of another lengthwise to make the walls, and we use mud between the cracks, just as you do when building your rock walls."

"Are these places you build and live in quite big Thorvar?"

"Yes, they are, especially the house of families who keep their cattle and horses in one end of the log building with them. As to size - well, I have walked your cave with long strides across the front and it took me about seventy two of these long steps (216 feet) from one side to the other. Many of our log houses are about twenty strides (60 feet) long. So we could only build about three of our long houses in your cave."

Nakota thought a minute and then replied, "They are very large - but I would not want so many people living in this one large room with me."

Thorvar started to tell him that this was not true, that only one family lived in such a building. But he decided not to do so.

"But you say that some have horses and cattle living in their large room with them. What is this you called cattle?"Thorar shook his head, smiled at him and said, "my friend, you ask too many questions. I am tired, I want to go to sleep. I will answer more of your questions another night."

They were up at the first light of day and climbed up some distance to where they had a better view. They searched the skies with no luck and could hear nothing stirring around the cave above.

Thorvar said, "Let's climb up to the cave and see what's there."

They started climbing over dead tree trunks and around large boulders, but every so often slipped backward when they tried to climb in loose, coarse soil. After a time, they began breathing heavily from the high altitude, and both were soon searching for a level place to sit down until they could breathe more easily.

Their slow advance up the steep slope was time consuming and the sun was high overhead when they finally reached a ledge just below the cave. After resting quite some time, Thorvar looking upward, said."That big cave above us seems large enough for a bird the size of that Devil Bird. Chances are that we will find his roosting place this soon only through the greatest of luck, but it certainly is worth checking."

Nakota nodded. They slung their long bows and arrows over their shoulders, checked their knives, and quietly climbed the remaining distance to the cave opening.

CHAPTER 8

T hey stopped about ten feet below the edge of the cave to listen. They were about to look up over the top of a large boulder into the cave, when they suddenly heard a loud noise in the cave and ducked back down behind the boulder. The noise became louder and nearer, as if something with claws was running on the cave floor. Just as it seemed to be almost upon them, there was a thunderous flapping noise and a very large object with tremendous wings struggled from the edge of the cave. It lifted into the air, and then began gliding swiftly down into the valley.

The two of them were so startled that they had little chance to look at this enormous bird, other than to see the great spread of its wings.

Thorvar, in awe, blurted out, "By the great God Thor, that bird's wingspread must be at least twelve feet. Never had I seen anything like that!"

Nakota, with a gasp, said. "I thought it was going to swope down on us. It must be the biggest bird anywhere in this land. It has to be the Devil Bird. It may return soon and see us."

"I agree. We'll hide in the cave and prepare to kill it on its return - the Gods willing."

So they climbed quietly up on to the cave floor and cautiously looked inside. Seeing and hearing nothing, they entered the opening of the cave. They sat down on several large rocks and immediately began readying their large bows and long, sharp-stoned arrows for the Devil Bird's return.

While they were doing this, they began hearing noises farther back in the cave. With bows and arrows ready, they sneaked along the far edge of the cave, back toward the area from where this disturbance was coming. They were startled once again when an object came flying through the air in front of them, barely above the floor, and after only a short flight, clumsily hit the floor. It was the last flight for this young condor bird, as two arrows pierced its body. Its wings, only partially covered with feathers, fluttered and jerked about and then the young bird became motionless.

Thorvar and Nakota were very cautious, thinking there might be a mother bird in the cave. As they slowly went toward the back of the cave, they saw a large feathered object lying on the floor. Two swift arrows quickly pierced this object, which remained motionless. When they came closer, they noticed it was about the size of the bird that had suddenly flown out of the cave. But they soon realized that they had not killed this one, it was already dead.

It had been killed recently by many sizeable rocks. Apparently, it was the female condor. They did not know this was a scavenger bird and they were amazed, as they remove the large rocks, to see how large it was, and how ugly.

Nakota exclaimed, "Look at its large head and neck, they don't have any feathers, just skin. And its ugly skin is all wrinkled and reddish-orange. Ugh!!"

Thorvar looked closer, "Yes, but look at the powerful beak and the huge claws."

Thorvar said. "We have no way of knowing how soon the Devil Bird will return. It might not be until late in the day or it might be very soon. We'd better figure out where to hide and be ready to ambush it with many arrows."

Nakota added, "Also, we need to see if there is another way out of the back of the cave, in case it blocks the entrance."

"Right you are. Why don't you climb up on some of these legdes and see if you can find places where we could hide and be out of its reach. I'll go farther back to where this narrows down and see if there is a way out."

Just as they were about to split up, several rocks came tumbling down from a high ledge above and several more followed. Immediately on the alert, with arrows ready to launch. Nakota called out, "Whoever you are, come down where we can see you or we will come up!"

A young voice replied, "Don't shoot! I will come down. I did not mean to hurt you!"

They stood with drawn bows while this person climbed down around the ledges and rock formations until he was standing near them.

He was a young, dark-skinned boyish person, which surprised both Nakota and Thorvar, but they were even more amazed to see how tall he was. He was almost as tall as the Viking and taller than Nakota. They lowered their bows and told him to come nearer.

"We won't hurt you," Nakota told him. "We just want to see you in a brighter light and find out what you are doing here."

He came cautiously toward them but with a look of defiance. "You best not hurt me or my tribe will hunt you down and kill you."

Again they told him they planned no harm. Then Thorvar asked him, "What is your name and where is this tribe you speak of?"

"My name is Natcha and I come from a tribe down in the valley beyond."

At the mention of the name, Nakota appeared startled, so much so, that Thorvar asked him what was wrong. Nakota replied, "That was the same name as the boy who was taken by the Devil Bird four summers ago. He would be about eight summers old now. But of course, he could not be our boy, Natcha, because he could not possibly be so tall."

The Viking shook his head and said, "No, Nakota, that could not be. Even your grown people are much shorter." He then turned to the youth and asked, "What were you doing up on the high ledge?"

"I was waiting there with many large rocks for the other large bird so I could kill it as I killed its mate earlier, while it was gone."

Both of them were completely taken aback by this comment and Nakota asked, "Why would you want to do this?"

"Because they are very bad birds and one of them brought me to this cave when I was small. Some people in my tribe found and rescued me and took me back to my home in the valley beyond."

"Did this large bird take other little children from the tribe in the valley?"

"No. But they say it tried several times."

At this point Thorvar interrupted, "Nakota, we can talk more of this later. Right now you and this tall young one had better hide and be ready when that Devil Bird returns."

Although Nakota was anxious to ask more questions, after some hesitation, he agreed. He and the "tall young one" hid themselves up on high ledges, Nakota with plenty of arrows but the boy with only his rocks.

After Nakota settled down in his "roost," he looked around to see where Thorvar was. When he couldn't find him, he called out, "Thorvar, where are you?" There was no reply. Again he called out more loudly, but still there was no answer.

Natcha shouted to Nakota, "I saw him walk out the front of the cave and disappear!" This distrubed the cliff-deller, he began to worry but then reasoned out loud to himself, "He has very likely just gone outside to see if he can sight the Devil Bird."

After more time passed and his friend had not reappeared, he decided to climb down from his ledge and go look for him. He could not find him in front of the cave or along the walkway side. It then occurred to him that maybe the Viking has fallen down the mountain, and as he looked below, indeed, did see him some distance below. Nervously he began climbing down toward him, loudly calling to him to stay where he was; that he was coming down to help him.

The Norseman gave a hearty laugh and called back up to him. "I'm not hurt. I just came down here where I could get a strong, straight tree limb and a stone to make a war club." Nakota reached Thorvar and saw that he was attaching a wedge-shaped stone near the end of a weathered, stout club-like piece of wood. He was securing it with sinew wrappings he had brought along as an extra bow string.

When he was asked why he was doing this, he replied, "I am going to stand up to that Devil Bird and kill him with my War Club." He then jumped up, swinging his new weapon overhead and roared, "I will not hide from it! Vikings do not hide from their enemy! We face them head-on and kill them in fair combat!"

As Nakota looked at his Viking friend, who was over a head taller than himself and observed his large strong body with wide muscular shoulders, and the look of fire in his eyes, he decided that maybe Thorvar could kill this large, ugly vulture with just his war club.

They climbed back up into the cave. Nakota crawled back up to his ledge, - but the Viking sat on the floor inside the cave, eagerly awaiting his enemy.

It was late in the afternoon when they heard a great beating of wings descending toward the cave. As the huge bird landed and folded it wings. Thorvar stepped forward where it could see him, and threw a rock to get its attention. The vulture, whose head was almost at a level with Thorvar's, turned its bald, ugly head around, sighting him. Thorvar then, to aggravate it further, threw more rocks with all his might, hitting it hard in the head with several of them. The bird stuck out its long neck, lowered its ugly head, and with its wing outstreatched and its large beak wide open, it charged. Thorvar, his war club held overhead and his knife in the other hand, stood ready. But just before it reached him, he swung his war club with great strength into the extended head. The vulture staggered, but the force of its charge knocked Thorvar down and it fell on top of him. Although stunned for the moment, its talons dug into Thorvar's left shoulder.

Pinned in this position and unable to free his left arm, he desperately tried to get the knife from his left hand. Letting go of his club, which was now useless, he finally succeeded in transferring the knife just as the huge bird was about to gouge out his eyes with its cruel beak.

The aroused Viking jabbed his knife viciously up into it breast. The bird instinctively reacted by momentarily rising, which permitted Thorvar to scramble out from under. He grabbed his club and swung viciously at its head, at the same time jabbing the knife repeatedly into its body. As the bird toppled over, it extended it neck and struck wildly with its beak. Thorvar swung with all his might, hitting it once more on it large, bald head, and thrust his knife into the featherless, orange-reddish neck with the death stroke.

Then he went over to the side and sat down on a boulder, holding his left shoulder with his right hand, which became covered with blood. Nakota and Natcha, who had been climbing down to help him, rushed over to see how badly he was hurt. By this time his shoulder was bleeding profusely where the talons had dug into him and it was very difficult for him to raise his left arm.

They both expressed great joy the Devil Bird and its family were all dead, but concerned for the serious bleeding and loss of strenght in his arm. Nakota quickly left but reappeared a short time later with some leaves and plants he had found lower down the mountain. He pressed these against the wounds and with one of his spare bow strings he tied them tightly in place, to stop the bleeding as well as to treat the injuries.

They then fixed a bed of branches of soft needles and had Thorvar lie down to conserve his strength. They found dry wood and made a fire in the front of the cave near him, as the night air in the high mountains became much colder. The next morning they were awakened by Natcha who talked excitedly about taking them to his tribe in the valley, so that their Medicine Man could heal Thorvar's injuries and make his arm strong again. However, Nakota decided that they must wait another day for Thorvar to regain more of his strength and then they would decide what to do.

CHAPTER 9

A s they sat in Ratum's small, separate cliff dwelling, some distance from the larger cliff dwelling, Cherko was shaking his head angrily saying, "If it hadn't been for that ugly, light haired one, I could have had that Ne No for my mate, to do the cooking and make my sandals and blankets. Then I wouldn't be cold at night and would not be hungry so often."

"But," replied Ratum, "We can still go ahead and steal her. That paleskinned, loud-mouth has been gone with Nakota for some time now. He says he's from a land far away, so he will likely never return."

Cherko shook his head saying. "I'd like to but they said that if I ever returned there, they would throw me off their highest cliff!"

Ratum sneared, saying, "That's if they catch you. They told me that too. But they are weak and afraid. All they do is dance and chant and pray to their Gods to help them. And with Nakota and that big paleface no longer there, we can easily steal her during the night."

"Yes, that may be. But how could we do it?"

Cherko thought awhile and then said, "Maybe we could get five or six others who don't have mates and are living along in caves nearby, to help us."

Ratum disagreed, "Naw, they wouldn't do it. They wouldn't get anything for it. Why should they help us? And beside, we want her for ourselves."

Cherko looked up angrily and said, "What do you mean - want her for ourselves? I want her for myself - not for you, too!"

"Well then, why should I help you?" sneared Ratum.

Cherko glanced out of the corner of his eyes, frowned and replied, "I think you will do it because of the way all of these people in the large cave treated you - driving you out. You'd like to get even with them somehow."

"Yeah! I'd sure like to show them up and hurt them some way. We will find a way."

They made plans and started the next morning on their trip to the large cave. By the time the sun had passed its zenith and was half way down toward the setting, they were settled into a hidden place on the canyon wall opposite the large cliff dwelling. There they began watching for Ne No.

She did not appear alone until dusk, when they saw her going down the path toward the spring with a large pottery bowl on her head. They watched her fill the bowl and sit for a while before starting back up the steep path.

Ratum whispered, "I wonder if she does this every evening alone? And why does she stay so long just sitting?"

They could not see from that distance that she was obviously with child and therefore it had become necessary to rest often.

Ratum said, "Let's stay here until tomorrow and then hide down there. Then if she comes down alone again in the evening, we can grab her, get up that ledge there, and then climb on up through that opening in the dead-end wall. It looks like that opening in the wall leads to a gradual rise on up to the top."

Cherko, finally beginning to show some enthusiasm, said, "Yes. And once we get on top we can keep going through the night, since the full moon will light our way. We can be a long way from here by the time they miss her." And so they bedded down for the night.

The next morning Ne No, who had had a uncomfortable night, was up early working on the cradle board for her baby. A little later her mother came by the door to her small room and noticed what she was making. She nodded her head and said, "Yes, Ne No. It is time you were beginning to prepare for your little one. But what are you doing, padding the head of this cardle board? You know it is necessary, that in order for your child to be flat at the back of its head and have broad face, it must rest against the hard wood of the cradle. If you pad it, your child will grow up to have an ugly, round head like Torvar's."

"That is exactly why I want to do it. So his baby's head will be round like his. Beside, I don't have to work in our fields where my baby would have to be strapped to the cradle board on my back. There is no need to protect its weak neck, since I don't have to lean and work in our fields."

"But Ne No, none of the other children have round heads. When the baby grows, she will be laughed at by the others."

But Ne No ignored her and padded the head board with a soft woven mat of cotton and turkey feathers. And just to make the padding a little thicker, she pulled out some of her own black hair, weaving it into the padding.

By the time Ne No had finished, she was tired and lay down to take a nap. She had been asleep for just a short time when she was abruptly awakened by something falling on her - and then another hit on top of her. As she quickly opened her eyes, she was confronted by two pairs of small, wide-open, startled eyes staring back at her. She quickly realized that these were two of her sister's children who had stumbled into her room while chasing each other. She grabbed them both, gave them a big hug, and sent them on their way. "After all," she thought to herself, "it won't be too long before I will have one running around like that."

She snuggled down with this wonderful, happy thought to complete her nap. But she couldn't get back to sleep. She kept wondering if Toe-war was safe. What if the Devil Bird killed him? When would he be coming home to her? Would he be coming home or would he stay in the mountains?

After the evening meal, she picked up her large pottery bowl and started down the path to the spring, as usual, to get water so they would have it ready when they arose the next morning. She liked to do this because it also gave her a chance to be alone and think of the happy times she and Thorvar had enjoyed in this lovely, secluded place.

Her pleasant memories were interrupted by a noise nearby, like rustling dry leaves back among the bushes. Her first thought was that it might be one of those grey-coated animals that were about the size of their larger dogs, but showed their teeth and snarled and were vicious. But when she heard nothing further, she decided that the momentary noise was caused by some small ground animal, like the little ones with the stripes down their back who scurried around hunting for nuts.

After she rested a little longer, she picked up her bowl and kneeled down to fill it from the pool. Suddenly she felt a hand clapped roughly over her mouth and a pair of arms grab her, pinning her arms to her body. Then she was roughly jerked to her feet by two men. One of them she recognized as Ratum and the other one looked vaguely familiar. As she wrestled to get free, she was dragged toward a ledge and hoisted up. She was not able to call out for help because of the hand clamped tightly over her mouth.

She struggled as they dragged her toward a large crevice in the dead-end wall. Then the one with his hand over her mouth encircled her shoulders with his right arm. while the other one grabbed her legs and they started laboriously up through the large crevice. Finally, after quite some time, they reached the top.

At this moment, weary from the climb, Ratum loosened his grip. Ne No immediately wiggled free, bumping hard against Ratum, which made him lose his balance at the steep edge of the canyon top. After quite an effort to regain his balance, swinging his arms wildly, he went over the side, shrieking all the way to the canyon floor below. As she made this sudden move, she too lost her balance and fell, tumbling part of the way down the crevice from which they had just emerged, She came to rest about a fifth of the way down, jolted against a large boulder.

Cherko, shocked by all that had happened so suddenly, started to go down the crevice toward where she lay. Then he changed his mind and started running from the canyon, to distance himself as much as possible, as quickly as possible, from the cliff dwellers.

Ne No lay there, perched against a large bolder, only half conscious. After a time, she began to regain her senses somewhat and started sobbing, not only from the pain throughout most of her body but the shock as well. After a seemingly endless time, she heard her name being called by people below in the canyon. They had heard the screams and had rushed down to see who it was, thinking it might be Ne No , whom they had seen going down for water. She called back a number of times and finally heard someone yell. "Ne No, where are you?"

She called back as loudly as she could, "I'm up here near the top of this opening!" She then passed into unconsciousness.

When Ne No awakened, she became aware of many voices chanting. As she opened her eyes, she realized she was in her Mother's room. Then she stiffened in great pain, suffering particularly in the lower part of her body. Her Mother and oldest sister rushed to her side.

Outside, the people danced in rhythm to their chants, in a circle around the fire. This continued through the night and as dawn arrived, Ne No's Mother emerged from her dwelling, and in tears said "Ne No is going to be alright. She does not seem to have any serious injuries, but she has lost her baby."

CHAPTER 10

T horvar was very restless during the night, mostly because of the pain where the Devil Bird had dug its talons so deeply into his shoulder. Nakota was not able to stop all the bleeding.

When it became apparent in the morning that Thorvar might not be able to travel for several days because of his weakness from the loss of blood, the tall boy became quite upset, saying, "I don't want him to die. We must get him our Medicine Man. He can help him."

Nakota admitted that his friend had a bad wound and asked, "How far is it to your tribe in the valley?"

"It is not too far, it is a small valley. Since our valley is surrounded by mountain walls, it does become dark earlier than up here. But I can easily get there before dark, unless I see some of our large, dangerous animals. Then it will take longer, for sure."

"Then it is not too far, but I still don't think we should risk moving Thorvar for another day or two, until I've completely stopped this bleeding and he is stronger."

The youth nodded his head and said, "Then I will get our Healer and bring him here." He turned and ran toward the rear of the cave, jumped down to a lower level, rounded a wall, and disappeared.

Thorvar and Nakota were both surprised to see Natcha disappear so suddenly out of the back of the cave. This aroused Nakota's curiosity and he said, "If you are alright for a little while, I think I'll go see what way he used to get out of here." Thorvar nodded, saying, "Yes, if we were suddenly confronted and needed an escape, it would be good to know."

Nakota placed the large bow and a number of arrows beside his friend and then he disappeared as Natcha had.

He jumped down to a lower level, rounded the wall, and found himself in a low, narrow passage. It was fairly dark and he was soon feeling his way along. He had to stoop lower and lower, and before long, he was forced to get down on all fours to crawl along this difficult passage. Now he was in almost total darkness and bumped his head as the passage made an abrupt turn to the right. He continued feeling his way along, but suddenly he fell.

He stood up, reached up to the level from which he had just fallen, and realized the abrupt fall had been only about the distance of his height. As he stood there trying to look around, he realized he was now in only semi-darkness because a little light shone through another opening in one side of this small pit. When he got down on his hands and knees to peek through this low opening, he saw just ahead of him a large chamber-like area with sheer walls extending forty feet straight down. He was pleased to see light coming down into this area from several openings high above. He crawled through this low opening onto a narrow ledge.

In order to get around the side of the large pit to the other side of the passage, he had to edge carefully sideways with his back to the wall. When he had eased himself about half way around, he noticed that a part of this narrow ledge was gone, and in order for him to continue, he would have to jump a long distance to the narrow ledge which continued to the other side of the gap.

He stood there trying to decide whether to attempt this jump or not. He looked far below and saw what looked like two skeletons laying on the bottom of the pit. One appeared to be an animal and the other a human being. The more he looked at these and the distance he would have to leap to the other side of this narrow ledge, the more discouraged he became.

He finally decided it would be a very foolish thing to attempt. If he didn't make it he would certainly fall to his death as those other two below had done. Then Thorvar would be left with no food or water and would have to try to make his way back down the mountain alone in his weakened condition. So Nakota decided to retrace his route very carefully. When he finally arrive back with Thorvar, he described his scary trip and expressed amazement and wonder at how the young Natcha had managed to do it.

The following morning, after some discussion, they agreed that it was extremely doubtful that the Medicine Man could or would come all this distance to treat his wounds. There was no way the two of them could make the leap safely from one side of the narrow ledge to the other side. In addition, the Viking's wound looked much better and he felt stronger. It was decided they would rest another day or two and then when he felt stronger, they would start back down the mountain.

That evening, Nakota put more dry wood on the fire and sat down on the opposite side from Thorvar. As the flames danced merrily across the top of the fire, radiating their warmth, with the dry limbs in the fire snapping and popping, both of them felt quite relaxed. They stared at the fire for quite some time, saying nothing, as if drawn by some hypnotic force.

Finally Nakota said, "Some nights ago, sitting around a fire like this, I asked you what a 'cattle' was, which you said sometimes shared one end of your long, wooden homes in your country. We were both tried and sleepy and you said you would tell me more about your country some other time. Can you tell me more about this now?"

The Viking chuckled and then said, "The cattle I mentioned are large animals we raise which give us a white, milky looking substance that we drink like water. Some are killed for their meat which is roasted over a fire and is very good to eat. What else would you like me to tell you?"

"I would like to know more about your homes and customs."

"Well, let me think a moment. In our country, the oldest man in each family is the owner of the home and is head of his family. This is unlike your custom where the mother owns the dwelling and is head of your clan. Since. the area where we live in Norway has a great many big trees, we used the wood to make and build our homes. We also use this wood to make benches to sit on and four-legged tables on which we serve our meat and other foods we eat. Long benches are put beside the walls, to sit on during the day and sleep on at night. At meal time the long tables are set beside the benches. We usually ate fish and drink milk one day, alternating with meat and ale the next day - very simple eating. Before and after meals, our women pass basins of water and towels. This is done because our hands become greasy when we cut off chunks of meat or fish with our hunting knives and eat holding the food in our hands. On special occasions we drink 'mead,' which is made from honey - it make us very dizzy and carefree."

The Viking mused for a moment, then let out a loud laugh, chuckled to himself a while longer, nodded his head, and said "I miss all that one hell of a lot. It was not unusual, when we got to feeling good, to do crazy things, like getting out of control and falling into the fire."

He chuckled quietly, then broke out laughing again, and with tears running down his cheeks, said, "And then we grabbed a bucket of mead and poured it all over a man, even if he wasn't on fire." He wiped the tears off on his sleeve, stared into their cave fire for a while and finally said, "I sure miss it!" After another pause, he looked over at his compaion and said, "Now - since I've told you about my country and some of our customs on at least three occasions, it's time you told me some of your history and more about your customs - some of which seem crazy to me."

Nakota nodded his head in agreement, stared into the fire for a time, deciding where to start, and then said, "Our Ancient Ones, years ago, lived in pithouses in the ground. They would dig a large, oblong hole in the ground with sharp rocks and wooden tools, until they could stand knee-deep in it. This shallow pit was used as the main room, with a similar, small antechamber attached, used as a storage room. Usually there was a ledge area dug along the base of the walls where people could sit.

"Then there were four holes dug in each corner of the pit for the posts that supported a roof framework. Small tree trunks were placed across the tops of the four posts. Small logs, as well as bark and sticks were crisscrossed to cover the roof framework. It was sealed with mud to help keep out the rain and snow.

"This oblong-shaped roof had walls sloping to the ground on all sides. These pithouses were entered by walking on the roof to an opening above the central fire pit on the floor of the dwelling. This, and a small overhead opening in the antechamber, let the air in and let smoke escape from the pithouse's central cooking and heating fire."

At this point Thorvar interrupted, saying, "Was this where the idea of kivas originated?"

"Yes, because these pithouses included features such as a small hole, we call it 'Sipapu', in the floor between the fire pit and the north wall, just as you have seen we now have in all our kivas."

"Why did you do away with this kind of home and move into your present dwellings in the cliffs?"

"Because when it rained hard, the water would run down into these pithouses. Also these places made of wood would easily catch on fire. Snakes and wild animals could get in easily and they were hard to defend against an enemy."

At this point, both men were suddenly alerted by a snapping of twigs nearby, and looking into the darkness, they saw two pairs of eyes staring at them. Thinking that they were wild mountain animals, possibly bears or mountain lions, Nakota quickly added more wood to their campfire. He made sure it was very dry wood, to get the fire blazing quickly with high, hot flames.

Meanwhile, Thorvar got his hunting knife and tossed Nakota's knife to him, as they prepared for a possible encounter. This bright, hot fire caused the intruders to back off somewhat, but the eyes were still looking directly at them, although from a slightly greater distance.

When this continued for some time Thorvar said, "I don't want us to have to stay up all night keeping this fire going to keep them away. There's plenty of moonlight to see by. I'm going to sneak back in the cave and work my way around to the other side, back of them, and see who and what they are."

After he had been gone a short time, Nakota heard his partner let out a big, "Haw - Haw - Haw." When he reappeared back by the fire he said, "It was just a couple of mountain goats." After he sat down and made himself comfortable by the fire he said, "Now, tell me more about your people."

Nakota put his knife down beside him, settled himself down near the fire once again, and resumed, "Because of the problems I just told you about, our 'old ones' next began building their homes attached in a semicircle to each other up on ground level. They used shaped sandstone rock walls, as we do now."

"But," said Thorvar, "I don't understand why your people then didn't continue to live in these rock dwellings on the level ground instead of living up in cliffs as they now do. Now you have to climb from the canyon floor to carry your water and also climb from your dwellings to get up on top to plant and tend your food crops. Also, it would seem that you would lose some of the privacy that you had in the earlier dwellings."

Nakota nodded his head, "These things are true. But by moving up into the cliffs to live, we made it more difficult for an enemy or wild animals to sneak up on us. We can now defend ourselves. Think back to the recent time when you helped us withstand the assault those cruel northern Indians tried. Could you have defended us successfully if we had been living in dwelling on the ground level?"

Thorvar nodded his head in agreement, "Yes, it would have been a great deal more difficult."

"Yes, and further, living up in our cliff caves we have much less sickness because we are away from the ground moisture from the rain and snowy winters. Besides being much drier, we are also much warmer in winter because our homes face the sun and the hot rays shine on us much of the day."

As the Viking changed positions sitting on the hard rock floor near the fire, he said, "There is one plant (yucca) that grows in this part of the country that puzzles me. It seems to grow best where the soil is very sandy and dry. It is everywhere - in the canyons, on top above your cliffs, on flat barren land. It is very ugly with its long, narrow spiny leaves, lined on all edges with very hard and sticky needles. It seems as if every time I'm not looking, it sneaks over and sticks me on the legs. I could do without this plant."

"Maybe you could, but we can't. We have too many uses for it. We use its stringy, long fibers in our sewing to make clothing, sandals, blankets, and as snares for catching small animals. Further, it is used to make soap, and the buds and blossoms are used for food. Those sticky needles you mentioned are used sometimes in sewing."

Thorvar stood up, stretched his arms overhead, yawned several times, "Well, now I know why you endure living in the cliffs and tolerate those sticky plants. Think I'll get some sleep now."

Nakota smiled and replied, "Me too." He fixed the fire for the night and soon both were snoring loudly.

CHAPTER 11

A fter two more days had passed, Thorvar had regained much of his strength. Also, the wound appeared to be healthy and beginning to heal. Since Natcha had not returned, they decided to start down the mountain the following morning. This was becoming a necessity after three days above timberline, since they no longer had any food or water, and the stench from the three dead birds laying in the cave was becoming obnoxious.

However, just as the sun was setting that evening, they heard a noise in the back of their cave and on looking around, saw Natcha emerge carrying two, extremely large dead rabbits, and some water in a bag.

When he threw them down on the floor in front of them, both looked in awe and Nakota said, "Those rabbits are almost twice the size of ours. Where did you find them?"

"I killed them in our valley on my way back to you." And then in a sad voice he said, "The Medicine Man said he could not leave our people to come this far to help you. But, if you will come to him, he will make you well."

Thorvar thanked him for his effort and told him that he was very much better, and that they were going back down the mountain toward their home in the morning.

Natcha seemed very disturbed when he heard this and said, "I am sorry I couldn't get back sooner, but I was forced to stay in the top of a very tall tree most of one day because three large wolves were stalking me below."

When Thorvar asked him how large the wolves were, he replied, "Well, when they were standing down on all four legs, their backs would have been a little higher than my hip bones."

Nakota expressed surprise that the wolves he described and the rabbits he had brought were so much larger than any he had ever seen. Natcha replied. "All the animals in our valley are large."

While Thorvar skinned the rabbits and started cooking them over the fire, Nakota told Natcha of how he had tried to use the same passage through the back of the cave and why he had finally turned back. He asked the boy how he had been able to jump across this gap in the narrow ledge safely to the other side.

"I didn't go that way. I took a much easier tunnel passage."
Nakota said. "I didn't see any other way."

"Of course you couldn't see any other way. It is very dark in there. How I always know when to turn into this other, easier passge is when I bump my head at the sharp turn. That's where you went the wrong way. Just to the left at that point is the passage I take. You went to the right. The one I took is easy to follow and comes out into the open above our valley, after a short distance."

Thorvar interrupted, "I'm eating these rabbits I cooked. You'd better come mighty soon or I'll eat them both myself, even if they are big!"

After they had eaten and the two men had quenched their thirst, the boy sadly asked, "Why must you go back down the mountain and return to your homes so soon? You have only been here a few days and the people in my tribe in our Valley were looking forward to you coming to our Medicine Man. They were curious to see both of you; one of you as a small-size man, but they especially want to see a man with white skin and blue eyes like the sky and really light-colored hair."

"So you told them of how we are strange and funny lookin, eh?" inquired Thorvar, looking out the corner of his eyes.

Natcha, looking a little worried, stammered a bit, and then hesitantly said, "Yes, - but I - well, also told them how you fought the Devil Bird and killed him almost bare handed. And I told them how Nakota stopped the bleeding right away and took care of your wound, where the big bird's claw dug into your shoulder.

"And - and - they want to see you both, the one man who, although little, was not afraid to seek out and fight the Devil Bird, and the strange looking man who, without arrows, fought and killed it. They wondered if you might be some kind of God - to go into its den, high up in a cliff and kill it single-handed."

Thorvar replied, "Well, you killed its mate. Do they think you are some sort of young God now?"

"Well, I haven't told them about it yet."

Nakota interrupted, saying in a demanding voice, "Why would you tell them I am a small man? I am bigger then most of our people. I am not small!"

Natcha squirmed a bit more and then replied "I guess I told them this because you are much shorter than any of them. Actually, most of them are even taller than Thorvar."

Nakota questioned this, saying, "Boy - you talk big! You say your wolves are bigger. Your trees are higher. Your people are taller. Why do you say these things that are not true?"

The boy became very quiet, as if deeply hurt and worried. Thorvar finally said, "Well, Nakota, maybe the boy isn't lying. He is as tall as you now - and is only eight or nine years old. These two rabbits he brought us are big. And we've never seen a bird as big as the Devil Bird and its mate. I mearsured the width of the Devil Bird's wings from tip to tip while you were exploring the tunnel, and it had a span of about five strides (15 feet). So - maybe he is telling the truth."

The youth rose upon his toes as high as he could stretch and said, "I am telling the truth. It is so!"

For a while no one said anything further, as they sat around the fire while night was beginning to settle over the mountain, each staring into the glowing embers, each lost in his own thoughts. The howl of a mountain animal pierced the silence. Finally, Thorvar shook his head slowly and said, "You know, what this young one says make me curious. I get to thinkin' that I'd like to see what really is in that valley of his."

He was silent a while longer and then asked, "Nakota, what would you say to us taking a few days and going down into the boy's valley and having a look? We might even visit his tribe for a day? I wouldn't mind a few more days in this mountain country and you could find out whether the kid's lying or not. It would sure give you something to tell your people, sitting around the fire when we get back to the cliffs."

This last comment caught Nakota's attention. He thought to himself, "It would be great to be able to tell my people about my adventures, as Thorvar has been doing, and about things they have never heard before - that is, if these things are true. My stories might be told by my tribesmen around their campfires for years and years to come."

It was decided they would get a good night's sleep and leave early the next morning to go down into Natcha's "Valley of the Tall Ones."

But all had difficulty getting to sleep. The Viking was thinking about getting down into the mountain valley, with the smell of the pine, the ripple of the mountain streams, and the whisper of the wind through the pines, all of which he loved and missed so much. Nakota was thinking of the attention he would get telling about the Devil Bird's death and about these new adventures they were about to undertake. Natcha thought about proving to his people that he was not lying about these two strangers and the Devil Bird's death.

CHAPTER 12

Because of their difficulty in getting to sleep, none of them awakened until the sun peeked above the horizon and cast its rays into the cave. They arose and followed Natcha into the narrow tunnel at the back of the cave, but only after each man had checked his bow and stone-tipped arrows, and Thorvar, his hunting knife.

They soon lost the boy as he hurried ahead. After a while, they were crawling on their hands and knees in the darkness. Nakota and Thorvar wondered if they could find the turn, but after bumping their heads, they, too, by carefully searching along the left wall, found the passage where Natcha had gone.

They had crawled only a short distance when they saw dim light in the low tunnel and, after rounding a curve, they saw daylight. They soon crawled out onto a wide ledge, high above the valley. They heard Natcha calling to them to follow. As they stood and looked down into this valley, it seemed to be as Natcha had said. It was fairly small, surrounded by steep hills and mountains walls. They looked to the far end, where they could see from their vantage point that this valley seemed to end abruptly in sharp rise, almost straight up, of hills and rock formations. Beyond this was a body of water, which appeared to be a very large lake, directly above the end of the valley.

They followed slowly down the mountain. They could see that this was a beautiful valley with much vegetation. Approaching the valley floor, Nakota and Thorvar were quite surprised to see that the trees were all unusually tall, as were the grasses, bushes and vines.

It seemed strange to Nakota, and especially to Thorvar, to be following the precautions of a mere boy, even though he was within his own surroundings and was very tall for his age. However, within the next half hour, they were both thankful that he had been cautiously leading the way.

As they followed a small mountain stream through a wooded area, they noticed that Natcha had stopped and was peering intently from behind a large bush. After a few moments, he looked back at them, put his finger to his lips cautioning them to be very quiet, and motioned them to follow him. He led them over to the side of the valley and they hid behind some large rock formations.

They had been there only a short time when they heard a noise some distance away, of something moving through the underbrush, which seemed to be moving towards them. As it came nearer and nearer, they peeked around the rocks to see what was causing this noise. Soon they saw a huge, furry, greyish-brown animal come from behind some trees, sauntering along on four powerful legs.

Nakota just gapsed, "It's as tall as me!"

Thorvar looked at the huge grizzly bear in amazement, "Never in all our mountain country of Norway have I ever seen a bear that size. He must be three big strides in length!"

Natcha whispered, "He is the most vicious and deadly of all the large animals in our valley, He has killed men in our tribe with one swing of his large paw. He may not notice we are here, since we are downwind from him. Also, his eyesight is such that he can not see too well."

They remained very quiet as the animal continued to advance rather slowly in their direction. The boy, upon hearing some small commotion behind him, turned and saw his companions placing long arrows in their large bows.

He shook his head, whispering, "No, you must not shoot arrows into him. If you do, it will not kill him. It will only make him very angry and he will rush upon us and kill us. Also, he can outrun us. We must pray to our Gods that he does not find us."

Thorvar, undaunted, continued to position his arrows and grabbed his hunting knife, preparing to fight.

Natcha seeing this, begged him not to act. "Please listen to me, Thorvar. I have seen two of our warriors, as great as you, killed quickly when they tried to fight this one." So Thorvar reluctantly agreed, as did Nakota, to use his weapons only if attached by this huge animal.

The beast was within twenty feet of them when he stopped, sniffed around and suddenly stood up on his hind legs and began eating some berries from a vine entwined about fifteen feet up in a tree. Thorvar and Nakota, who had drawn their bows in readiness, gasped as they saw this enormous animal towering above them - three times, at least, as tall as Nakota.

It was soon apparent to each of them that this monster was not yet aware of them, but only as long as they were very quiet and the wind didn't shift. For the time being all they could do was watch him and pray that he didn't come any nearer.

He stripped the berries from the vine with his mouth and some of the berries fell from his mouth to the ground. As they watched, they noticed several small animals with grey stripes down their backs, quickly scurry out of a hole in the ground near the base of the tree trunk and hurriedly gobble up the berries the bear had dropped. They were scooting back and forth, sometimes running across the bear's feet. Annoyed by this, the grizzly growled as he dropped down on all four paws and began trying to catch them.

In spite of the serious position in which they were trapped, the three of them couldn't help but be amused as they watched this enormous bear, hindered by his poor eyesight, trying to catch the two small animals as they squeaked and scampered about, avoiding his massive paws. Finally, when he realized they had ducked into the hole by the tree, he began trying to dig them out. While he was intent on this, the small ones scampered out of their other hole on the other side of the tree trunk and collected the rest of the berries just behind him. The grizzley tired of digging after a few minutes, wandered over to some large bushes nearer where the three of them were hiding, and began eating berries again.

Suddenly he stopped, raised his head and looked directly in their direction. Thorvar and Nakota braced themselves as they drew back their bows across their long arrows, ready to strike. The bear continued to face their direction, swung his head slowly back and forth - and after what seemed to the men an infinite period of time, slowly turned around and ambled down to the stream, lapped up some water, and disappeared among the trees.

They stayed put for some time and then cautiously went to the stream and resumed following it toward Natcha's village. They continued to be on the alert as they traveled, since now they were beginning to believe some of the things that Natcha had told them. Even the little animals that had irritated the grizzly as they scampered around for the fallen berries were almost half again as big as their similar stripe-backed little animals who stayed near the spring of their cliff dwellings.

Although the three of them moved along cautiously, keeping themselves alert in this beautiful but unusual valley, they did not see any more animals until the sun was directly overhead. They saw a pack of wolves, trotting away from them. These wolves, even at such a distance, impressed the Norseman with their unusual height and size.

Natcha stooped by the stream to hand-cup a drink of water, and as the other two came up to him he said, "We have to move along faster to reach my tribe's camp before dark." After they had covered quite some distance, Thorvar and Nakota noticed that they were gradually going uphill toward what appeared to be the end of the valley in the distance. The two men also noticed a roaring sound, and as they rounded a large wall of rock, they saw a waterfall. It dropped into a fairly deep and narrow gorge, which ran in front of them, then veered off to the left carrying the water from the falls around a sharp curve and into the valley below.

What really caught their attention was that just to the left of the falls, across the gorge, was a wide deep rock-shelf. At the back of this was a large cave - about half the size of the cliff dwellings, but with a much lower ceiling. They also noticed a group of men, women and children, all of unusual height, doing various things on the flat rock shelf.

As Thorvar looked straight down into the gorge and then at the tribe's location on the other side, he turned to Natcha and said. "This is all quite amazing - how do you get over to your people?"

Natcha smiled, "This place was chosen because it was hard for the animals in the valley to bother us. Come, I'll show you." It was obvious to the men that this was a moment of pride and importance to the boy. They followed him along a path at the edge of the gorge until the path turned to the left and came up beside the waterfall. Natcha motioned to them to stop and in a loud, high-pitched voice, speaking about the noise of the water he said, "There is a ledge that goes just back of and under the falling water to the other side. The water will not hit you - you will be behind it. But the ledge, which is not very wide, will be wet and you will need to move slowly and carefully because - well, just because." He quickly disappeared into the mist. Thorvar and Nakota felt their way down too and eased along this ledge. Thorvar, exhilarated by this new challenge, started moving boldly ahead. Just as he did, his foot nearest the edge went out from under him on the slippery surface and he grabbed wildly about for one of the bushes growing out of the rock wall. He grabbed one just as his other foot slipped out from under him and suddenly he was dangling over the side of the ledge, hanging onto the bush for dear life, with nothing but a deep gorge below him.

In spite of great effort, he could not get either of his feet back up over the ledge. His legs were dangling too far below. Nakota, close behind, instead of panicking grabbed hold of another bush, carefully pulled on it testing how secure it was, and then with the other hand managed to remove his large bow from his shoulder. He then very carefully hooked one of Thorvar's feet, securing it between the end of the bow and the bow-sting and gradually Thorvar got one foot up and with a mightly effort, was able to pull himself back on the ledge in a sitting position.

Natcha, who had crossed to the other side, became concerned when they didn't show up and was about to back-track, when they appeared out of the mist.

"Are you alright? The seat of your pants is very wet, Thorvar. Did something happen?"

Thorvar hesitated and then started to explain, but Nakota hastily said,

"No. Nothing special happened." Then he quickly changed the subject with, "Look, here come several men from your tribe."

The 'boy' in Natcha then came into full bloom as he ran over to the two men, and began talking excitedly to them in a language that neither Nakota or Thorvar understood, pointing back several times in their direction. The two tribesmen approached with slow and measured strides until they stood in front of their visitors.

Natcha proudly pointed at his two friends, "This is Thorvar and this is Nakota." Each of his tribesmen, in turn, reached out and placed his right hand first on Thorvar's left shoulder, and then, after a little hesitation on Nakota's, bowing very slightly as they did so.

When they again stood up straight, Thorvar noticed that both men were a good head taller than himself - and Nakota winced a bit as he realized they were at least two heads taller than he was.

One of them said something to Natcha in a loud voice above the roar of the waterfall, and he in turn relayed the message, shouting. "Wa'Sho and Wa-Gu-er'o say you are to follow them. They will take the hurt pale-face to their Medicine Man, Wa-Yam'pa." With that understood, they turned and with heads held high, led them over to the flat rock shelf in front of their cave.

CHAPTER 13

T he Indian men and women, whom Thorvar noticed were almost all taller then he was, stood silently but respectfuly as they passed among them to a small cave entrance beside the large cave. Some looked in awe at the man who was pale skinned with strange hair and eyes. Several snickered as they looked at the "little man" who walked beside him. They were stopped just short of the small cave entrance. They stood there while the two tribesmen went inside. After some time, they emerged following the Medicine Man. He was a tall, thin older man with white hair hanging down around his shoulders. He barely glanced at them and then turned, crushing some scented leaves in his hands and ceremoniously spread them across the entrance to his cave. After this, he looked up to the heavens, twice let out a piercing cry, and then slowly turned to the two tribesmen and motioned to them to let the two visitors enter.

After Thorvar and Nakota entered his cave, their guides introduced them, and then left. He stared into the eyes of Thorvar, then looked down at Nakota - and then back at Thorvar again. He continued staring at them for some time and then, addressing Thorvar, pointed to himself and began saying something which, of course, the Viking couldn't understand. He repeated it and when he realized the pale man didn't know what he was saying, called Wa'Sho.

When Wa'Sho brought Natcha to act as interperter, the Medicine Man repeated what he had said. Natcha turned to Thorvar, "Our Medicine Man says that he is Wa-Yam'pa, the Great Healer. He wants to look at the wound on your shoulder." He then looked at it rather casually and told the boy who repeated, "He says it is almost healed. It must have been a mere scratch." Both Nakota and Thorvar left, disgusted.

It was not until later that they learned that these people were not only tall, but also proud and did not normally welcome strangers whom they thought were not their equals. The two guides were certain that the very short one was inferior but they were puzzled about the pale-faced stranger with the almost colorless hair. The people among whom they had passed were also silent because they were awed by the big chested, white faced one who was almost their height. They have never seen anyone like him.

After this partial snubbing by their 'Great Healer,' Wa'Sho and Wa-Gu-er'o decided they were not of much importance even though the young Natcha thought they were. Wa'sho told them to sit down on the rock floor.

They started not to do so, but decided they were a little tired and maybe it would feel good to sit a while. They sat there resting while the two guides, who had stepped off to the side, argued with each other. Soon Natcha wiggled his way in between them, and finally was able to say some things. But Wa-Gu-er'o soon pushed him aside.

Thorvar, after some time, motioned to the youth to come over to them and asked, "Natcha, what are they arguing about?" "Oh," he replied in a disgusted manner, "They are arguing about what to do with each of you. Whether you both are worthy to approach their two Chiefs or whether they should just get rid of you both, since Wa-Yam'pa almost totally ignored you both. I told them that Wa-Yam'pa was just jealous of the way Nakota had healed your bad wound. and that he was afraid of you, Thorvar." He frowned and said, "Wa'Sho wants to talk to the Chief but Wa-Gu-er'o wants to throw you both into the highest part of the waterfall."

Thorvar started to rise, saying, "Well, we'll see if he's man enough to do it!" But Natcha pleaded with him not to, pushed Thorvar back down, and quickly turned and ran into the entry of their large cave, as Wa-Gu-er'o tried to stop him.

In a short time Natcha reappeared, followed by a man and woman, both nearly seven feet tall. Wa-Gu-er'o started to intercede but the tall woman motioned him aside. Nakota and Thorvar got to their feet. As the people started to gather, Natcha, feeling very important, introduced their two Chiefs, Wa-Kan-e-ach'e and his wife, Wa-Ka-chi'na. Very proudly he said, "This is Thorvar, who faced and killed the Devil Bird alone, with only his club and knife. And this is Nakota, who also came to kill this terrible bird, and who quickly healed the deep shoulder wound Thorvar received from the sharp claws of the big bird, the one who stole me from our home and tried to swoop down and carry away one of your little girls." And then the youth rose up on his toes and shouted, "These two men, alone, got rid of that awful bird. You don't have to worry about it any more!" The women all began to cheer - but the men were silent.

Wa-Ka-chi'na put her hand on both of Thorvar's shoulders and Wa-Kan-e-ach'e, after some hesitation, did likewise to Nakota. They bowled their heads toward their guests and the people crowded around, laughing and talking since their Chiefs had accepted these two strangers.

Each of the Chiefs then said some words to them which they, of course, could not understand. They looked at the boy and he happily said, "Our Chiefs say you are most welcome and wish you to come into the large cave to rest after your day-long journey."

As they entered, they were surprised to see what a large cave it was. Wa-Ka-chi'na said something to Wa'Sho, who told Thorvar and Nakota what she had said, But of course, they did not understand Wa'Sho either. So Natcha was summoned again and he relayed the message. "She told Wa'Sho to make the visitors feel welcome and fix a place in one of the small, inner caves where you can both rest from your travels. She also told him to bring you food."

When Wa'Sho and several women had laid out pads for them, they sat down and began looking around. This large cave had a high domed ceiling with many small inner-caves as well as deep indentations around its perimeter. It became obvious as they looked around, that these smaller caves were for families, giving them privacy as well as protection from the weather.

After Thorvar lay down to relax, he heard a murmuring sound, like water running over rocks. He got up to investigate and found a miniature waterfall flowing into a fairly large basin-like rock section in the floor. From there it drained, much as an overflow, into a smaller narrow crevice almost half way up the side of the basin. Thorvar called Nakota to come see this constant supply of water inside the cave. Nakota said, "They don't have to go down in a canyon and carry up water. Our women would like that. They have running water, fresh water, right up here where they live. When we get back, we had better not tell them about that."

Then they began guessing where the water came from, and Thorvar said, "I imagine it comes from the lake that is right here, just above their beautiful waterfall. It runs right down through some cracks in the rock." Natcha agreed and said, "And the water goes out that crack half way up the basin and drains down into their canyon out front." As they continued to look around, they noticed a rapidly decending passageway. As they were about to investigate, Wa'Sho and Natcha (Thorvar noticed he was being called, Wa-Natcha) came with their food.

Natcha remained with them while they ate, so Nakota asked him, "Where does that passageway on the right side of this big cave go?" The young one happily replied, "It goes down to a dark cave, fairly large one, under our lake and waterfall. I will ask permission of Wa-Kan-e-ach'e and Wa-Ka-chi'na to take you there tomorrow."

Both men were expressing their interest when Natcha interrupted saying, "Oh, I almost forgot. Our Chiefs want you to sit around the big campfire in front of the cave this evening to visit. Also, they want you to tell them how you killed the Devil Bird and where each of you comes from."

They agreed they would tell a little about such things, but Thorvar said, "They speak a different language, how?"

Natcha interrupted, saying, "Oh, I will tell them what you say."

Then Nakota said, "Sit down here boy. I want to talk to you." After seating himself in front of the young one he continued, "Until we reached this tribe, we thought they would use the same language as ours, since you immediately talked to us in our words when we first found you hiding in that cave." He looked the boy straight in the eyes and said, "How can you understand and say things in our words?" The youth looked a bit frustrated, flustered a bit, and then stammered, "I - I - don't know, they just come to my mouth - and I understand."

Nakota hesitated a moment and then quietly said, "You know what I think?"

The boy looked down at the cave floor and replied, "No."

"Well, young friend, I think that you are our long lost Natcha that the Devil Bird took from us. How you got to be this tall, I don't know. But I think you are our Natcha."

To the surprise of both Nakota and Thorvar, the boy did not deny such a possibility. After a silence he looked up and asked, "If what you say is true, would I have a mother and father back where you say I came from?" Nakota smiled and reassured him, "Yes. And they would be so very happy to have you back with them."

The boy smiled ever so slightly and mumbled, "Would they really want me and have me live with them?" After he was reassured by Nakota, he grinned a little wider and said, "That would be nice. I have no mother or father here. The other young ones here don't like to play with me. They say that when I was young I was very short. So they think something must have been wrong with me." And then, with his head held high, he said, "But now I have grown to be as tall as they are and they still don't pay much attention to me."

Nakota faced him with a hand on each of Natcha's shoulders and quietly inquired, "Natcha - would you like to go home with us when we leave in a day or two?" Natcha looked a bit puzzled, hesitated, and then replied, "I - I - I will think about it."

Just then a tall youth rushed in and told Natcha, "Our Chiefs say you and the strangers should come see them now!"

CHAPTER 14

A t the entrance to the Chiefs' inner cave, Natcha stopped and lowered his head, at the same time indicating to Nakota and Thorvar to do likewise. The two Chiefs were seated on rock benches on a wide shelf one step above the inner cave floor. Just behind them was an opening in the wall, much like a window, which provided a beautiful view of the waterfall and the valley below. The woman Chief, Wa-Ka-chi'na, rose and motioned the two strangers to step forward. Then Wa-Kan-e-ach'e, also rose, and stooping down from their higher level, they placed their hands on Thorvar and Nakota's shoulders. This time neither bowed - but motioned both to sit on the edge of the higher shelf, facing the Chiefs.

Wa-Kan-e-ach'e, after clearing his throat, announced with a degree of arrogance, "Our Medicine Man, Wa-Yam'pa, and our greatest warrior, Wa-Gu-er'o, and some of our other warriors said they will permit you to sit at their campfire tonight, but they do not want any of you to tell of where you came from, which they say, is of no interest to them. Further, they do not believe the boy, Wa-Nat-cha's claims that you, Pale-face, killed the big Devil Bird. They say you could not have done this because there are two, not one, of there very large and vicious birds who live high up in the mountains. You would have had to kill both of them at the same time. No ordinary warrior could do this alone. Wa-Gu-er'o said it would even be difficult for him. So you may sit by our fire tonight, but you must say nothing." Having finished this edict, Wa-Ka-chi'na, followed by her mate, quickly moved and sat down on the ledge beside the two visitors, and in a very friendly voice, began talking to Thorvar. He, a bit confused by this sudden change of attitude from one of superiority to one of quiet friendliness, turned to Natcha, inquiring about what she was saying.

The Chiefs then directed their questions to Natcha, who, after some time listening to their questions, turned to Thorvar and Nakota and said, "They say they are interested in where you came from and is it true that you, Thorvar, fought and killed the Devil Bird?"

Through Natcha they visited with the two Chiefs, answering their questions and telling of how both Devil Birds and their offspring were killed. The chiefs were inclined to believe Thorvar's feat, but not that Natcha killed the female bird.

Then, in turn, they answered some of Thorvar and Nakota's questions, confirming that Natcha was not originally of their Tribe but had been found in the Devil Birds' cave while they were away. He had been brought back to their Tribe and kept at the Chiefs' insistence. Wa-Kan-e-ach'e then explained, "These big birds are not normally able to fly and at the same time, carry anything in their talons. They must eat off of dead animals that they find. Since this one was so much larger, and his talons were so much bigger and stronger than the others of his kind, this Devil Bird would be able to fly and carry Natcha, as a small child, to his cave."

Thorvar's next question was, "Why are all of you so very big and tall?"

Wa-Kan-e-ach'e thought on this for a moment and then, with interruptions so that Natcha could relay what he was saying, replied, "Our Gods have given to our Mother Earth in this valley, very special `gifts' (abundant amounts of nitrogen, potash, phosphoric acid, and iron in the soil) that make her very generous."

"But how?" asked Thorvar.

"These `gifts' from our Mother Earth make all the trees, the grasses, the bushes, the berries, nuts and the plants grow tall and have much strength within. We, of our Tribe, as well as all the animals big and small, apparently gain strength and bigness from all of the foods we eat. Wa-Natcha has so benefitted. It may also be that when we eat the animals we kill in our valley, we may gain strength and size from them. I do not know."

Nakota interrupted saying, "But how did the Devil Bird get so big and strong? They do not eat anything but the meat from dead animals." The Chief, a bit irked, replied, "I do not know this either. Maybe they benefit in some way by drawing on the strength of the dead animals who ate these plants, grasses, berries, and nuts. Again I say - I do not know. Only our Gods who gave these `gifts' to our Mother Earth, would know."

Thus, Thorvar and Nakota learned a little of this beautiful valley's secrets. The two friendly Chiefs, in turn, were told much they did not know about other lands and peoples.

As they were about to leave their inquisitive hosts, Thorvar asked one final question, "Why do you have two Chiefs?"

"Wa-Kan-e-ach'e replied, "I am chief of the warriors. She is chief of the women." And then he smiled and said, "And of me."

And as they turned to go, he called to them and said, "You are welcome to stay tonight and tomorrow night to rest before continuing your travels!" He paused, and then said, "After that it would be best that you leave. And in the meantime, stay away from the other warriors after our campfire tonight, especially Wa-Gu-er's. And, oh yes - you who call yourself `Nakota' - stay away from Wa-Yam'pa too. He is very jealous of your apparent healing powers." And then, in her firm voice, Wa-Ka-chi'na added, "Things are peaceful now. We want no trouble."

That evening, Thorvar and Nakota had both decided not to go to the campfire because of the warriors' snubs and attitude. At first, Thorvar wanted to go and if necessary, fight Wa-Gu-er'o. Nakota convinced him, that since the Chiefs had been friendly with them, and they would soon be leaving, they should not cause trouble with the tribe. Nakota reminded the proud Viking, "Remember, the Chiefs said they want no trouble. They want to keep things peaceful."

Thorvar said, "I will listen. It is best."

They built their own fire in the inner cave. Thorvar looked at the fire for a while and said, "Natcha, how about taking us down that passage over there that goes into that dark cave under the lake?"

They each lit a torch from the fire and Natcha led them down into this mysterious cave, carrying their weapons.

CHAPTER 15

They had gone only a short distance down the steep passageway when they suddenly emerged into a large cave with many unusual rock formations. As they continued on into the cave, Thorvar and Nakota were amazed to see all sorts of rock formation - some hung like large inverted cones from the low ceiling, and some rose from the cave floor. Others were like slender columns extending from the ceiling to the floor. Still others were formed like bunches of grapes. As they slowly proceeded further into this cave it felt damp and cool, and they could hear water slowly dripping. Thorvar thought he also heard a sound like someone moaning further back in the cave's darkness. He stopped and listened intently but did not hear it again. He decided it must be from wind passing through some part of the cave. He resumed looking here and there as their torch light revealed all sorts of unusual glittering rock formations. One resembled a frozen waterfall.

Again, Thorvar thought he heard someone moaning weakly. But when Natcha and Nakota gave no indication of hearing this, and when he heard nothing more but the echoes of their footsteps and dripping water, he dismissed it once more.

Continuing into the dark cave, lit only by their torches, they saw many more slender formations hanging from the ceiling, looking like icicles colored in soft tones of amber and lilac. Nearby was a resemblance to a cascade formed by white rock (onyx). Some smaller and more delicate formations resembled flower blossoms.

Suddenly, from back in the darkness, a long, shrill wailing sound startled them. Nakota stumbled backwards, dropped his torch, and as he fell bounced off the base of a large cone shaped formation protruding from the floor. He just missed impaling himself on its sharp pointed tip. Both men were somewhat shaken for the moment, but as Thorvar helped his friend up from the floor, Natcha seemed unconcerned. As they looked inquiringly at Natcha, he said, "Oh, it is nothing - no danger to us. It is just one of our people who is fastened to a rock column. They do this as punishment leaving them in the dark without food."

Nakota replied, "In this very dark and damp cave - and without food? How long do they keep them here?"

"Well, it depends on how bad they were."

They had been so intent in looking about that they had not observed another torch light entering the cave. This torch was extinguished shortly after entry. They had also not heard muffled and stealthy footsteps slowly approaching, moving from behind one rock formation to another

Nakota, as he picked up his torch, which was still lit, looked at Natcha and pointed, "Show us where he is and we will release him."

Natcha hesitated and looked at Thorvar, who shook his head saying, "No, Natcha. We should not interfere. Maybe the Indian deserves what he is getting. We might bring him some - -.

Thorvar never completed the sentence as a large body, pounced on his back, knocking the torch from his hand. Simultaneously, strong arms encricled his neck and began choking him. Thorvar struggled violently to get at this person on his back. But weakened by the weight of this large body, and being unable to pull the long arms from around his throat, he, in desperation, began searching for some immediate answers.

As they struggled, he suddenly remembered the sharp cone-shaped rock formation that Nakota had almost fallen on. Desperately, he tried to see where it was. He finally saw it some distance away. He called upon all his strength in this crouched position, and, gasping for breath, was able to inch over near the large, shape, pointed cone. Then, with a might heave, he turned himself around, placing their backs to the spear-like stone and fell backwards onto it with the full weight of both bodies.

A loud scream of pain pierced and echoed through the cave, as the arms released from around the Viking's neck. As the echoes rebounded about the walls of the cave, Thorvar rolled free and lay on the floor gasping for breath. When he recovered some of his breath, he got up, grabbed Nakota's torch and looked down on his attacker. He had managed to raise himself off the point of this cone, although it had sunk deep and he was weak and bleeding. As Throvar looked, trying to see who it was, Natcha exclaimed, "It is Wa-Gu-er'o, our greatest warrior."

Still trying to regain his breath, Thorvar quickly found a large rock and was poised to bash in his adversary's head, when Nakota yelled, "No! Thorvar! No!" He was still trembling from his temporary weakness, but in his Viking fury, he paid no attention and raised the large rock high over his head. It slipped backwards out of his trembling hands and fell on the cave floor behind him. It bounced away from him and as he turned to retrieve it, Natcha picked it up and ran into the darkness.

Just then Wa-Gu-er'o let out a loud yell for help. Soon afterwards someone yelled something back, the voice apparently coming from the upper entrance. Nakota looked at Natcha, "What did he yell back?"

"He shouted, `Stop your yelling and screaming Wa-Kun'da. We will free you tomorrow. Be quite `til then'." And then the youth added, "He thinks the yelling and screaming is coming from one who is being punished here, Wa-Kun'da. I am glad he did not come down to see."

Thorvar, now having recovered his breath and logic, pulled both his companions off to the side away from the injured one and quietly said, "I would like to go back up into their cave and face them, but with so many, it is not wise. Natcha - is there another way out of this lower cave? We could use this night for travel before they discover this sneak, Wa-Gu-er'o, in the morning."

Natcha quietly replied, "Come with me. I know a way out of the back of this cave. No one else knows about it."

Nakota and Thorvar started to go with the youth. But Thorvar turned back to Wa-Gu-er'o, sneared at him and said, "I should kill you - but only when you can fight back. I don't sneak up on people from behind, like you do." Then he started to give him a vicious kick in the ribs - but changed his mind and walked away.

As he departed, Wa-Gu-er'o rose up on his elbows and shouted after him, "I will follow and kill you!!" Then he slumped back down as he passed out. Neither one really understood what he had shouted at the other, but from the loud, threating tones of voice, they knew that their conflict would resume some day. Then Throvar joined his two friends, made sure they all had their weapons with them, and with torches, followed Natcha into the darkness toward the back of the cave. This enchanting cave with its beautifully sculptured rock formations, gifts from Mother Nature, all created by lime and other mineral deposits in drops of water, falling for centuries like a slow and endless rain.

When the three of them reached the very back of the dark cave, Natcha turned to the right into a low, narrow tunnel. He cautioned them to move slowly when they rounded the next turn, since it would come to an abrupt end. When they cautiously made this turn, they held their torches high over their heads and saw that this underground tunnel suddenly did end, with a quick drop off. Extending their torches out ahead of them to see down into these depths, they observed a narrow subterranean stream, flowing swiftly by. In the shadows they could see it round a curve, flowing through the tunnel on a lower level.

While standing there looking down, Natcha said excitedly, "At about the time of the last full moon, since none of the other kids wanted to play with me, I decided to light a torch and go exploring in the back of this cave. As I rounded the curve, I fell off the edge right here, into the water below. As I stood up in the water, which was up to my shoulders, I was very scared. My torch had been put out, and it was very dark. I began to really get worried as the water began pushing me along.

"I tried to grab hold of something - anything. The water forced me along, bumping my head on the low rocks overhead. When the rock ceiling came down so low that it pushed my head underwater, I thought I was going to die."

Thorvar interrupted and said impatiently, "Alright- but you can tell us this later. Right now I want to know if we can get out of the cave this way."

"Yes!" replied the boy.

"Well then, let's get on with it before they trap us here!"

Natcha quickly explained what he had done to escape. They each had to drop a distance of about twice Thorvar's height, feet first, into this underground stream. They moved along with the flowing water and when the overhead passage was about to force them under water, they quickly took deep breaths. When they emerged a short distance downstream, they saw daylight peeking through a narrow opening ahead of them.

Natcha had cautioned them that shortly after they emerged through this opening, the stream would become a small waterfall, dropping sharply for some distance. With this in mind, they scrambled to a ledge as soon as they passed through the low opening.

They sat on the ledge for a while to dry out and recover their breath. Thorvar began observing the countryside that stretched out in the distance to determine which direction they should go once they were out of these mountains. As he looked toward the setting sun, he gasped as he saw the radiant sunset that was forming among the clouds over the distant mountain peaks. Some of the clouds were like islands in the sky, with brilliant silver edging encompassing every inch of their shore lines. Soon the islands seemed to float away and in their place, rays of gold radiated into the heavens from behind other clouds like the ribs of a great and beautiful fan. Their rays reflected against the bosom of Mother Nature's higher, fluffy clouds, as they seemed to drift through the sea of clear blue sky all around them.

Entranced by this gorgeous spectacle, Thorvar forgot all else, enjoying to the fullest this overpowering beauty in the heavens. After a bit, returning to reality, he realized that although it was still fairly light at this higher altitude, that twilight was beginning to settle in the foothills.

"We have to move down this mountain as far as we can before it becomes too difficult to see where we are going. But, thank our Gods of Thor and Odin that there will be a full moon tonight! We must travel as far as possible away from this `Wa' tribe of the tall ones before tomorrow morning, when they discover their warrior Wa-Gu-er'o, lying there in the cave."

He dangled his legs a little longer, looked over at Nakota, smiled and said, "Not that I'd mind fighting them - but I'd like the odds to be a little more even." After taking one final look at the beautiful sunset, he dropped down off the ledge, and, followed by his two companions, started a rapid descent. After they had picked their way down around boulders, bushes, and trees for some distance, Thorvar waited until the others caught up with him. Then he said to Nakota, "My good friend, I've been thinking about our upcoming trip across the desert back to our cliff dwellings. I know that we would like to get away as quickly as possible from these mountains because we may be followed. But we must find water and a little food to take with us before we leave these mountains and start across the desert."

Nakota replied, "It will be hard to find these things in the dark. We should have filled our water baskets while we were sitting by the top of the waterfall. The stream is now far to the right of us." Thorvar nodded in agreement, "Yes, it would be far out of our way now."

Thorvar put his arm around his friend's shoulders and said, "Well, it looks like the best thing to do now is go down as far as we can during the night until the moon sets behind those peaks. Then, when it is too dark to travel, get several hours of rest, and at the first light of dawn, search for water and food for the three of us."

Nakota agreed and said, "We need that rest after the long day we have just finished, traveling through that strange valley, then at the `Wa tribe's' cave, and now with the trip into the desert facing us tomorrow."

The three of them resumed their descent in the darkness, aided only by moonlight filtering through the tree tops to guide their way. Thorvar and Nakota remained constantly alert for large cats that prowled during the night looking for food. They did hear several howls and what sounded like coyotes, but they were off in the distance.

Quite some time later they noticed that the moon was about to go down behind the peaks, and in this much dimmer light they began searching for a protected place where they could rest until dawn. They soon found a thick rock shelf protruding from a large outcrop. After building a small fire of dry twigs to keep any animals away, they settled down, well back under this thick rock shelter.

The young Natcha could not get to sleep and when Nakota realized how restless he was, he asked, "Are you alright, boy?"

"Well, I've never slept on a mountain side, out in the open like this. Are you sure no animals will find us and eat us?"

Just as Nakota was about to reassure him, the ground under them began to tremble. As Thorvar quickly sat up, the ground began to shake more violently. At the same time they heard, some distance above them a rumbling sound that grew louder and nearer. Nakota and the boy started to run out from under the rock ledge to see what was happening. Thorvar yelled, "Don't go out there! Come back under this ledge, quickly!" They looked back at him in bewilderment. He yelled again, "Get back in here now!!"

Just as they ran under the ledge, the noise became very loud and rocks and boulders came thundering down the mountain, crashing against trees and bushes, bounding wildly around their shelter on all sides. Many boulders also crashed down on top of their thick, rock ledge, before ricocheting forward in their wild flight, crushing everything in their path. Other large rocks and boulders below them, dislodged by this powerful force, also joined the downward sweep in front of the three wide-eyed, but safe, onlookers.

They watched in awe as the tremendous force destroyed all before it. At the same time, they were trying to maintain their balance as the ground shook beneath them. The tremors began to subside, and soon all became quiet except for the rumbling and crashing below them, which quickly faded away in the distance.

When Natcha started to go outside to look around, Thorvar again yelled at the boy to come back in. As he looked back at Thorvar from outside, he heard a noise above him and saw several large boulders starting to roll down toward him. He dove back under the ledge before they came crashing down, just missing him.

As the smell of dust and the spicy fragrance of crushed needles and torn wood from the evergreen trees settled down around them, the bewildered youth exclaimed, "How did the `Wa' people know that we were here?"

Nakota, although still short of breath from all the excitement, said, "Yes! And how did they make the earth shake and the rock and boulders roll down toward us?"

After Thorvar regained his composer, he said, "The `Wa' people could not have done this."

The two, almost as one, asked, "But how else could this have happened?"

Thorvar was quiet for a little while, as if collecting his thoughts, and then said, "I remember a time while I was still a young boy, like you Natcha, back in my country. A similar thing happened in our mountains. Many people were killed and others seriously injured by falling rocks."

"My father said it could be caused by very large rocks shifting deep within the earth. Others believed it was caused by something from the sky crashing down to earth, causing the ground to shake." The Viking paused and then continued. "My father strongly believed it was Loki, half God and half devil, who caused this as one of his many vicious and cruel way to get attention and force himself into the company of our Gods."

Nakota replied, "Maybe the Chiefs of the `Wa' people got their Mountain Gods to do this to us." As he said this, they felt more tremors but after a few moments all was quiet again. They tried to go back to sleep but couldn't, and as the first light of day dawned, they went to see what damage had been done. All of them were amazed by the complete devastation above and below them. No trees or bushes remained in the path of the boulders. and large rocks were strewn over the area below as far as they could see.

As Nakota looked at all this, he exclaimed, "Thorvar! I think the gods of the `Wa' people really did do this. See how all the rocks above and below us are a direct path to us? Over there, on the other slope, there is not nearly as much damage, and very few trees were knocked down."

The Viking had noticed this too and said, "Well, whatever the reason, let's move over to the left, where it will be easier to climb down the mountain."

CHAPTER 16

C ollecting their bows and arrows, their knives, and their empty food and water baskets, they began their slow and difficult climb over the wide strip of rocks and downed trees. After they reached the side of the avalanche, they were able to resume their descent.

Nakota hurried on ahead, anxiously looking for water, which they would need on their trip. Natcha hung back to help Thorvar, who was collecting berries, nuts, and digging for roots to eat on their trip across the desert flatland.

They were also keeping a wary eye out for bears or large mountain cats that might have been disturbed by the avalanche. They were also looking for rabbits or squirrels that would make especially good eating. Suddenly they heard a call for help from quite some distance away.

They hurried in the direction of the call, and in their rapid descent, crossed a path made by deer or other animals. They ran, following the path along a deep ditch. Thorvar, who had outdistanced the boy, made a sharp turn around a large boulder and almost fell over some large rocks scattered across the path. After regaining his balance, he yelled back to Natcha, "Look out for the large rocks in the path just around this big boulder!!"

As he waited for Natcha, he heard a call from the deep ditch below him, and looking down saw Nakota hobbling along, holding on to the side of a shelf of rocks. He was bleeding on his forehead and both elbows.

"Are you badly hurt?" Thorvar asked anxiously.

"No - although I'm shaken up some. But I guess I did twist my ankle rather badly." Then he explained, "I thought I heard running water up ahead, and in my hurry to see where it was, I ran around that boulder too fast, stumbled over those rocks in the path, and fell headfirst down here."

When the boy arrived, Thorvar told him what had happened and then said, "Natcha, we've got to get him up out of there, but the side of the ditch is too steep. Climb up in that tree over there and cut off that big vine hanging down from it. Here's my knife." When this had been accomplished, they lowered one end of the vine to their bruised friend, and the two of them pulled him up onto the path.

When he tried to get up and walk he experienced difficulty and after sitting back down, Thorvar looked at his ankle, carefully bent it back and forth, and said, "It's not broken and the sprain doesn't seem to be too bad, but it is beginning to swell." He raised his eyes to Nakota and said, "You were quite right about hearing water running nearby. Natcha, run on ahead and find the water. I'll carry our friend. We need to get his foot and ankle into cold water as soon as possible."

The youth looked puzzled and said, "I'll find the water right away, but how is washing his foot and ankle in that water going to help his ankle?"

Thorvar smiled and said, "It will stop the swelling and he will be able to walk sooner."

Natcha shook his head and replied, "If you say so. But it doesn't make any sense to me." And with that, he was off and running down the path.

Fortunately, the small stream was not too far away. They followed the trail to a hollow where a lazy mountain stream flowed into and out of a small pool of crystal clear water. It was obvious to the Viking that this was a drinking hole for mountain animals, since the trail came right down to it. Also, this small hollow was fairly well hidden by the trees and bushes on the banks above.

Thorvar lowered Nakota to the ground and helped him hobble over to the pool. After Nakota sat down and placed his foot and ankle in the deepest water, he looked up at his companion and said, "This water is really cold."

"Yes, you can move it out of the water now and then when your foot and ankle get numb from the cold, but keep at it. This should keep the swelling down. It will surely numb the pain."

The boy sat down beside them. Thorvar gave each of them some roots and berries to eat. He washed the roots off in the sparkling water, looked up at them and said, "You know, I was just thinking that this might be a good place to spend the rest of the day and night. It is well hidden, just in case any people from the caves of the `tall valley' might be hunting for us. They couldn't get here before tomorrow.

But the boy said, "Since you think this is a watering hole for animals, aren't you afraid that those big mountain cats that prowl in the night might come here to drink while we are here - and find us?"

The men agreed this could happen and decided they should keep a fire going during the night. And so, after eating their abbreviated meal and drinking from the fresh mountain stream, the Viking said, "Well now boy, I think you and I had best get busy finding more food for our trip across the flat land." After placing Nakota's bow, arrows and knife beside him, they disappeared up the hillside into the woods.

When they returned just before dark, Nakota was pleased to see that their food baskets were filled with many berries, nuts, and roots, and two rabbits were hanging from the tall boy's belt. Thorvar looked at his friend's ankle and exclaimed, "The swelling is mostly gone. Now I will sit you close by the fire and you can keep your ankle near the heat of the fire off and on during the evening. Maybe tomorrow you can walk on it and we can leave." He showed his companion a walking stick he had made and said, "With the help of this, you should be able to walk at least to the bottom of the mountain tomorrow."

They ate and refreshed themselves from the pool once again, threw more logs on the fire, and soon were sound asleep. At dawn they were suddenly awakened by movement close by and saw two deer and a fawn drinking from the pool. As they sat up, the deer shied away, but soon returned to their drinking when the men sat quietly, watching them. However, when Natcha moved all three deer turned quickly and disappeared up the bank.

After they had eaten, Nakota tried walking with the aid of his new crutch. He walked well enough to resume the downward trip.

While the men were filling their water baskets, Natcha sneaked up the bank to see if the deer were still there. Just as he peeked through the low bushes, he saw an arrow pierce the side of one of the deer and it fell to the ground. Then another arrow whined through the air and the female deer also fell limp to the ground. The suddenness of all this startled the tall youth, but what concerned him even more was that he recognized the three tall men who were approaching. They were from the cave of the "tall valley."

Natcha quickly slid down the embankment, ran over to the two men, and said in an excited whisper, "They are here. They have found us!"

Thorvar, trying to calm him down said, "Who are you taking about? What do you mean?"

"It is Wa-Kan-e-ach'e, our chief. And Wa-Kun'da, the one who was tied up in the cave, and another."

Thorvar, closely followed by Natcha, climbed quietly up the bank, peered through the bushes, and then boldly stepped out in the open, bow and arrow drawn, and called out, "We came to your cave with no intent to harm anyone. We will now leave in the same way. If you do not agree - one of you will die with me."

All three looked around quickly, obviously startled by Thorvar's sudden appearance. Natcha repeated to them what Thorvar had just said. Two of the three fell to their knees immediately and bowed their heads toward Thorvar. Their Chief, still standing, quickly recovered his composure and with the assistant of Natcha, replied, "Friend Thorvar, we intend no harm for you. We are quite surprised to see you again. We thought you had gone back to your clan or had traveled farther back into your mountains."

The Viking shook his head, "After what I was forced to do to your champion, Wa-Gu-er'o, I am sure you have been hunting for us for revenge, even though I had no choice in defending myself."

"No, my friend, we already have forgotten that. Wa-Kun'da, who is kneeling beside me now, told us what really happened. He saw it all while tied nearby in the cave. I can only say I am very sorry you were attacked - you were our guests."

Thorvar, taken entirely by surprise at this turn of events, looked at Natcha and said, "Ask Wa-Kun'da if this is true."

Natcha replied "Yes, he says this is true. He says, `Yes, O Mountain God, it is so. You were attacked from behind. You had to defend yourself as best you could. We have forgiven you all except Wa'Sho and his evil friend, Wa-Gu-er'o"

Thorvar looked back at the Chief and said, "Then why are you three and several others I now see approaching-why are you here? Why are you here, if not to seek us out?" The Chief replied, "We have had a terrible thing befall all of us. Two nights ago, in the middle of the night, our cave and the hills all around us began to tremble and shake violently. Great cracks opened in our cave, much rock fell around us and suddenly with a great roar, the walls that had held back the lake crumbled and the water roared down into the gorge and on down into the valley below.

"And as big cracks in the walls of our home cave widened the water which had been flowing through our cave flooded across the floor and we had to leave.

"We rushed down into the lower cave to untie Wa-Kun'da. This is when we found Wa-Gu-er'o lying on the floor by the large cone rock. His bleeding had stopped but his back revealed the serious injury he had received. We were deeply puzzled and very angry when Wa-Gu-er'o, told us about your cowardly act, sneaking up on him and throwing him against that sharp rock. However, when Wa-Kun'da told us what really happened, the man we had considered our champion admitted his guilt - but still swore his vengeance."

At this point Wa-Kun'da interrupted, saying, "We now know you are the White God of the Mountains. No one could have so easily conquered our champion warrior unless he was a God. Your skin, your hair, your eyes, your strength must be those of a God. No one else we have ever seen looks like you."

The Chief nodded his head in agreement, saying, "My people are convinced that you, as the White God of the Mountains, also caused the earth to shake, the water to flood, and our cave to become unlivable, in vengeance to Wa-Gu-er'o."

In the meantime, Nakota hobbled up beside Thorvar. He told them that Thorvar was not a God, but a man from a far away country where most people looked like him.

Thorvar agreed, "I am not a God. As Nakota says, I came from a country across a very great body of water, just as I told you and your other Chief in your cave two nights ago. It is as I told you." Then he told the boy to ask why, if they weren't hunting for them, were they here now?

The chief replied, "Because of the terrible curse forced on us two nights ago, we must now find a new home _ some other place to live. Our cave is flooded by the lake's water."

After Natcha had relayed this to Throvar, the Chief continued. "Our valley, which has always supplied us with meat and food, is now flooded by the lake, which will rise as time goes on. The animals that were not drowned will be forced to leave our valley. We will no longer have the abundance of meat and plant food nearby. We will have no cave shelter. We must move. So we came here to gather meat and other food for our journey."

Thorvar expressed his great sorrow for them and said, "Please tell your people that we had nothing to do with the terrible shaking of the ground. If we had not been under a rock shelter that night, we would have been killed by rocks rolling down the mountain." He took his knife from his belt, and standing where all of them could see, as he cut a gash across the back of his left arm, he said, "See, I bleed like you! I am no God, just a man like you, with different colored skin, hair and eyes. See? I bleed! I am no God!!"

As the tall men huddled together, Nakota hurried away, but soon returned with moss and large leaves, which he bound tighly around Thorvar's fresh wound with a sandal thong. The Chief approached Thorvar and said, "If you are not a God, you are at least, a very great man. If you say you did not cause the great shaking of the earth and cave, we believe you and will tell our people."

He motioned to one of his people, who came forward and presented Thorvar with a large piece of meat from one of the deer they had slain. The Chief then said, "You are our friends. Take this food with you for a safe journey to your homes." Then the tall ones turned and quickly disappeared into the trees and bushes up the mountain.

This unexpected turn of events caused Thorvar to say, "Since we now know that we won't be hunted by the 'Tall Ones' we don't need to hurry to leave these mountains. Nakota, we should stay here at least another day for you to rest and heal. We also need to eat this deer meat they have given us, since the warm days of travel across the dry land to our cliff dwellings would spoil this meat." And so it was agreed among them to delay another day.

Part of the reason Thorvar had given for their delayed departure was true. The other part was his reluctance to leave the mountain country that reminded him so much of Norway.

While Nakota rested, Thorvar took the tall boy by the hand and said, "Let's go exploring in these mountains. We'll leave these nuts and other food for Nakota and for our trip home. You and I can fill our bellies on what we find today."

The large, muscular, blond man and the tall, thin, black-haired youth went off across the mountain, enjoying the beauty of the mountains, the views, and each other's company.

The young one ran ahead, while Thorvar began looking for some small, pretty stones to take back to Ne No. Now that their mission had been completed, Thorvar could enjoy the fresh mountain air, the smell of the pines, and the beauty around him. He found himself thinking about the pretty, graceful Indian maiden, who was his lovely mate.

As he looked for different kinds of small rocks, he found some of granite, some that sparkled in the sunlight, and others that reflected the mineral colors of red, green, silver, and gold. He thought back on the time when he had first arrived in the cliff dwellings.

He recalled with a smile how the young, persistent Indian maiden had placed the wet, mushy substance on the wounds on his aching head. And how, when he angrily grabbed it from his head and threw it aside, she gently but firmly placed it back on his forehead and said in a quiet but certain voice, "Na Na" She had stayed there through the night, replacing the poultice now and then, and making sure he did not remove it again.

He thought of the hot days when he and Ne No had gone down the trail to the nearby spring, and after bending down to get a cool drink, they sat there and talked of many things, enjoying each other's company. She had asked so many questions about his home, and the things he did when he was a boy.

Then his thought turned to the arrival of their baby and he wondered how Ne No was feeling. When he left she seemed to be carrying the baby very well, and he even grinned when he recalled feeling the baby kicking within her. The kicks were strong, he was sure it would be a boy.

After they had gone down the hillside for some distance, they paused by a small stream to rest and drink. Natcha went into the nearby woods to gather some berries and a few edible plant leaves, When he returned he sat down by Thorvar and gave him what he had gathered.

"Do we have to leave these mountains? I like it here. Let's stay here."

"I'd love to stay here too, boy. But I've got a mate back at the cliff dwellings who is very special to me. She's going to have our baby soon. I need to get back there." Then, he put his arm around Natcha's shoulder and quietly said. "And I'm sure you want to get back to your mother and father, don't you."

"I suppose. But I don't really care. I'd rather stay with you."

"Oh no, Natcha. Much as I like you, your parents have not seen you for over four years. They think you are dead. They will be so happy to know you are alive and will be so glad to have you back with them."

The boy hung his head and said, "I suppose so."

After spending the rest of the afternoon exploring the mountain, they returned to Nakota a little before dark. He was cooking the deer meat, and with this and the other food they had gathered, they relaxed, enjoying a quiet companionship.

Nakota's ankle was much better so they decided that the next day they would go slowly down the mountain and the day after they would start out across the flat land toward the cliff dwellings.

The next evening, when they reached the flat land, Nakota's ankle was much better. The following morning, with their water and food baskets full, they began their trip home. The days passed without any unusual happenings and as they camped out on the final night, they could see their high, green mesa. Home was only about a half days journey.

CHAPTER 17

By noon the next day they had left the hot, flat countryside and entered the cool, shaded canyon leading to their cliff dwellings. They walked slowly under the limbs of the large oak trees, and as they approached the quiet nook just below the cliffs, Nakota and Natcha flopped down on the ground to drink the refreshing spring water. Thorvar hurried on up the path to find Ne No, whom he had thought so much about during the past few days.

As he reached the cliff dwellings, he noticed that no men were about, and all the older children were also missing. This seemed odd to him because at this time of day they were usually making blankets for the coming winter, or moccasins or tools or snares. He noticed that when he appeared at the top of the trail, the women working at their chores, looked up at him and then dropped their heads in silence. This also seemed strange, no greeting, just silence.

He hurried to his dwelling, but Ne No was not there. He found Ne No's mother, who replied to him while hanging her head, "She sometimes goes down the canyon. She has been painting pictures on the canyon walls there. If she is not there, she sometimes hides herself in that empty, small room on the second floor of one of our front dwellings."

Thorvar knew where this empty room was. He had slept there often on cool nights before he and Ne No were mated. He hurried to the front, climbed the weakened ladder to the second floor, pushed aside the cloth covering the door opening, stuck his head in and quietly sighed as he said, "Ne No, I have missed you so much. I am home."

Ne No was standing, painting a design on the back wall of the room. She turned quickly and rushed over to him. "Oh Toe-war, I am so glad you are home. It has been horrible it - -" and then she burst out crying.

He grabbed her in his arms as she buried her face in his shoulder. As he caressed her lovely black hair he said, "Ne No, what is wrong?"

She sobbed, tried to say something. Sobbed some more, and then managed to blurt out, "Toe-war, we have lost our baby!"

He was silent for a moment and then asked in a soft and gently voice, "It's all right, Ne No, but I'm awfully sorry. How did it happen?"

As she told him between sobs, of what had happened the second night after he left, his anger began rising and he said, "I remember that loud-mouthed Ratum. I am glad he died from the fall. He deserved even worse.

But which is the other one you call, Cherko?"

After wiping away her tears she said, "He is the one who, not long after you came here, tried twice to kill you while you slept - once with a rattlesnake and once with a large rock."

"Where is he now? Did they catch him?"

"No. Tanoto and four of our men, including my oldest brother, Nonacho, searched for four days and nights, but they could not find him."

"Where is Tanoto now, and all our other men?"

"They are with men from all the other cliff dwellings nearby, building a temple to the Gods (Sun Temple, Mesa Verde). They say that it will take some years to complete, but they are doing it together."

"Why are they doing this?"

"They do it to appease the Rain Gods in hope that more rain will fall." She hesitated, and then said, "Toe-war, you may not know this, but for some years we have been getting less and less rain each year to grow our crops. We must have plenty of rain to grow corn, beans, and squash. These are necessary for us to have during the cold winter months, when we can't find and kill enough deer, rabbits, and other animals. During the winter it is also hard to find herbs, roots, and plant food. All dwellers in cliffs around here have the same problems."

Thorvar, interested in what she was saying, but more concerned with revenge on Cherko at the moment said, "I will question Tanoto and your brother about this murderer, this evening when they return. I will look places where they have not looked." As he clenched both fists and raised them high over his head, he exclaimed in a loud voice, I must and will find this devil of a man, Cherko! He shall die!!"

Ne No, rising on her tiptoes, reach for his neck, rested her head against his chest and said, "I must tell you, they will not be home tonight. They have all decided to work two days 'til dark and sleep one night there each week while the weather is fairly warm, at least until time to harvest our poor crops. The older children are watching the fields up on top to keep any deer, birds, and rabbits from eating what crops we have growing."

Thorvar put his arms around her, kissed her and quietly said. "Then I must go now to learn where they have already looked for this Cherko."

Ne No snuggled closer and said, "Toe-war, don't leave me tonight. I need your strength to ease the sorrow of losing our child."

He looked down into her pleading eyes and said, "Yes, I want to be with you. But tomorrow I must go."

They sat on the floor, his arm around her shoulders, content to be together again. After some time, he asked, "What were you painting on the wall when I entered?" He got up and went over to look at it. "It looks like three X's inside a square."

"Well, Toe-war, that is what it is. One for you, one for me, and one for our lost baby" (still visible in this room at Spruce Tree House).

In their sorrow, they had not realized what was occurring on the main floor of the large cave. They decended the ladder and saw the women gathered in various groups excitedly talking to each other. Ne No said, "I wonder what they are so excited about?"

They approached the nearest group. One of the women rushed up to the Viking and in tears, said, "Oh, thank you, Thorvar, for bringing my Natcha back to me. But is he really my Natcha? He is so very tall for his age, and he doesn't seem to know me. I am not sure it is he."

"Well, Nakota seems to think it is Natcha. He speaks your language fairly well. The people he has lived with in the Shining Mountains the past four years are all very tall, almost a head taller then I am. I'm sure Nakota will tell you about this around campfire when the men return tomorrow evening."

Natcha ran up to Thorvar and pleaded, "Thorvar, I want to be with you. I do not remember any of these people. I think I remember a little about the cave, but I'm not sure. I've been in lots of caves."

Nakota overheard what the boy was saying and offered. "Thorvar, I do not have a mate. The boy can stay with me tonight if he wishes, until the men return."

The woman replied, "This is good. We will wait until tomorrow evening and see what my man thinks."

Nakota nodded his head and replied, "After I tell about the Valley of the Tall Men tomorrow night, it may help your man to understand. And the next night I will tell you about the Devil Bird we found. It may take many campfires for me to tell all that occurred in the Shining Mountains."

That evening, when they had finished eating, Ne No became curious as to who the tall thin boy was. Thorvar explained only briefly, "Nakota will tell more about what occured while we were in the Mountains, a great deal more, I am sure."

The next morning at daybreak Thorvar was up grabbing something to eat and preparing to go where the men were building the temple to appease their Rain Gods. When Nakota and Natcha learned why Thorvar was leaving so soon they wanted to go with him.

He replied, "No!" This is something I must do alone."

After finding out where the temple was being built, he gave Ne No a hug, picked up his bow and arrows, his knife, climbed the cliff to the top, and disappeared.

CHAPTER 18

Thorvar headed south on the mesa beside a deep canyon, winding his way among the low-lying pinon and juniper trees. In his haste, he brushed against the spiny, sharp needles of several yucca, causing him to bleed. But he hurried on.

It was a beautiful day and in the fresh early morning air, many birds could be heard singing their happy songs. In the distance the sound of the "caw, caw" of crows drifted in. But Thorvar was not aware of any of this. His whole intent was on finding the Indian who had caused Ne No so much heartbreak.

The sun was still fairly low in the eastern sky when he saw a number of men sitting on large pieces of sandstone, talking. As he approached them, he noticed Ne No's brother, and wound his way among them toward where he sat. Many of them looked up in amazement at seeing the large, white skinned man with the yellow hair and strange eyes.

He gave no notice of them and hurried over to Ne No's brother, asking, "Nonacho, where is Tanoto?"

He rose as he told the Viking, "He is that way where we are building the temple to our Rain Gods. It is on a point of land overlooking the canyon where one can see down into it from many directions. It is not far."

Thorvar replied, "Good, Can you go with me?"

"No, I must stay with these men, who have come from many cliff dwellings. Each of us is carrying a large stone to where Tanoto and others are building the temple. We could not keep up with you as you run, and besides, we are resting now."

As soon as Thorvar had left, a number of the men rose from where they had been resting and surrounded Nonacho, asking, "Is he the White God who says he comes from some far away land, the one that we have been hearing about?"

"Yes, he is the one. It is he, with the great imagination, who has told us strange stories in the evenings around our campfire."

They gathered, away form Nonacho, and talked for some time. They then returned to him, saying, "Maybe he is a god who has placed a curse on us and is forcing our Rain Gods to make so little rain for us."

"No," he replied. "He says he is not a god. He has helped us defend ourselves and our dwellings againts an attack by vicious Indians from the north. He has been a good friend and is mated to my sister, Ne No. Besides, he has only been with us from the last time of the hot sun, through one cold and snow time up to now. Our rains have become less and less for many summers, long before he came among us."

As Thorvar approached the men building the temple, he was surprised to see the size and detail of the structure. The foundation was about ten layers of sandstone. There were walls laid out for many small rooms on two sides and one end of the temple. The foundation included a group of small rooms at the other end, built beside an enclosed round room. As he wandered around looking for Tanoto, he noticed a large, round structure near the center of the inner area. He wondered if it might be a kiva at ground level. He walked behind the large, round formation, where three of the workmen huddled together, each holding an arrow loosely strung in his bow, arguing excitedly. As he approached, they turned with their bows drawn, facing him.

Thorvar raised his open, right hand toward them and said, "I come in peace. I am from the cliff-dwelling near the large spruce trees where Nonacho, Tanoto and Nakota live. I am looking for Tanoto. Have you seen him?"

They just stood there looking at him. They had never seen such a man before. At this moment, another man came around the circular structure, carrying a large rock. He quickly recgonized the standoff and said in a loud voice, "Do not be afraid of him. He is Nakota and Tanoto's friend, whom we have talked about. He is called Thorvar. I have heard him tell stories of a far-away land, while I visited their dwellings."

One of them lowered his bow and said, "He says he is looking for Tanoto."

"Is this so?"

"Yes, I wish to talk to Tanoto."

The newcomer nodded his head, "Then I will get him for you."

Soon Tanoto and three other men arrived. Tanoto rushed forward, grabbing Thorvar in a hug around his waist and exclaimed, "Thorvar! I am so glad to see you my friend. Did you complete your mission? Is Nakota alright?"

"Yes, the Devil Bird will bother you no more. Nakota is fine. But I need to talk to you about this Devil Man, Cherko, who caused Ne No's baby to die."

Just then they were interrupted by one of the men. His hair was greying and his face was thin. He spoke with obvious authority, saying, "Tanoto, who is this man with the colorless skin and burned hair? Should he be allowed here on this sacred ground where we are building our temple to the Rain Gods?"

Tanoto briefly told him about Thorvar, as Nonacho had done earlier in the morning. The older man, after listening intently, said, "Very well. But what was this `mission' you ask him about?"

Tanoto respectfully replied, "Oh, wise one, do you know of the Devil Bird that has swooped down and taken away little children?"

"Yes, he did this to one of ours while we were working in our fields. We built a wall along the front of our cliff dwelling so our little ones could not fall into the deep canyon below and be killed. But then this bird swooped down and carried away one of them and flew away with him toward the Shining Mountains."

"Oh Wise One, the mission from which this man has just returned was to find the Devil Bird's nest in the Shining Mountains and kill him. He and Nakota, whom you know, went on this mission together."

The old man turned to Thorvar, "If this is so, did you find and kill this Devil Bird?"

"Yes, I did. His mate and offspring are also dead. You need fear them no more."

After a little pause, the old one looked at Tanoto and said, "Then I must know this strange looking man. He must be a great warrior and we must soon have a celebration dance to honor him and Nakota."

Tanoto, with a sudden feeling of great importance, turned to Thorvar, "My friend, please meet Wu-Pot'ki, `the wise one' from a cliff dwelling planned and improved by his direction that is the safest place from attack of all our cliff dwellings. It is very safe because it is built on a ledge in a very high cliffs," (Balcony House, Mesa Verde).

Thorvar bowed, "I am very please to meet you, wise man. Now I have urgent need to talk to my good friend Tanoto, concerning the where abouts of the evil one called Cherko."

This drew Wu-Pot'ki's attention and he inquired, "Why are you interested in this man, Cherko and why do you call him the `evil one'?"

Thorvar looked over at Tanoto and said, "I was gone when this brutal thing happened to my mate, Ne No, and I do not know exactly how it came about. Please tell this wise man and the others while I listen. I want to know if what I have heard is true. If so, then I will continue my search until I find him and kill him."

Tanoto told of how Cherko, with the help of Ratum, sneaked around in the twilight and seized Ne No. He told of their climb, her fall, and the loss of her baby, while Thorvar was away seeking the Devil Bird. He also told of Cherko's two earlier attempts to sneak up on Thorvar in his sleep, trying to kill him.

When Wu-pot'ki had heard these things, he turned to the Viking and asked, "Is all of this true?"

He looked the old man squarely in the eyes and said, "Now you understand why I must kill him, no matter how long it takes to find him."

Wu-Pot'ki motioned him to sit down and then said, "You will not have long to search. I know where Cherko is, or was, just two sunrises ago. He came to my people's cliff dwelling seven sunrises ago, asking for protection from some enemy who he claimed was dangerous and was following him. He said he needed a place to hide and that our dwellings offered him the safest place, the most difficult to reach. We believed him and his story of no wrong doing."

The old man then told him how to get to their cliff dwellings, stressing that he would have to go back along the mesa top to the canyon next to this one.

Thorvar replied, "I thought your cliff dwelling was that one, on the other side of this canyon. (Cliff Palace, Mesa Verde), but I now realize it will take more time to get to yours."

Wu-Pot'ki nodded, "However, if you leave now and go the way I have told you, you should get there before dark. Then you may rest in our fields above the cliff tonight. You will find some food you can pick and eat. In the morning, while the rising sun is shining into our cave, follow the path down into the canyon below our dwellings. Once you reach the level below our cave, call to our guard of the ladder and tell him that I, Wu-Pot'ki, have given you permission to have the ladder lowered and to enter through the tunnel into our cliff dwelling area.

"When you have climbed the ladder, tell our guard your reason for seeking Cherko. Tell him that I, Wu-Pot'ki, direct him to show you where Cherko is hiding." After a moment of hesitation, he took a necklace with a greenish-blue stone from around his neck and place it around Thorvar's, saying, "This will be proof that I have given you this permission."

CHAPTER 19

T horvar thanked the "Old One," climbed over the outer wall, and quickly disappeared.

Following Wu-Pot'ki's direction, he turned north, back in the direction from which he had come earlier that morning. By the time the sun was directly overhead, he had reached a place where he could cross over on the plateau to the other side of the canyon. He then started south and a little east toward the rim of the next canyon.

Late in the afternoon he reached the top of the cliff dwelling and found the trail that would take him below.

His first impulse was to go down the trail and seek out Cherko. But he decided to heed Wu-Pot'ki's advise and wait until morning. He would be rested and would have the benefit of the sun shining directly into the dwellings while he searched for Cherko. He reluctantly sought food and a place to rest in their grain fields above, and as daylight faded away, bedded down for the night.

He woke often throughout the night, anxiously awaiting the sunrise. When it finally arrived, he found a place to hide his bow and arrows. After checking to be sure he had his knife in his belt, he started the descent.

When he had gone down for some distance, he looked back up toward the cliff dwellings and was amazed to see how high up they were in the sheer canyon wall.

He finished his descent and looked up again. A loud voice from above asked, "Who are you? What do you want?"

"I am Thorvar from the cliff dwellings with the spruce trees below; the dwellings of Nakota and Tanoto."

The voice called, "Come where I can see you better." Thorvar did, and when the small muscular man above saw him, he said, "You are strange looking. You do not look like either of them. I will not lower the ladder."

"I know I look different, but I have lived with them in their dwellings since the last food crop. I am their friend."

"I have only your word on this. Where is Nakota or Tanoto to tell me if this is so?"

"They are back working on the temple to the Rain Gods with your man, Wu-Pot'ki. Wu-Pot'ki said to tell you that he gives you permission to lower the ladder so I may come up to your dwellings."

The guard above replied, "Again, it is just what you say. Have you any proof that Wu-Pot'ki has told you this?"

"Yes, He gave me this necklace with the greenish-blue stone as proof." After some hesitation, the guard called to someone nearby. They talked awhile and then together lowered a long ladder.

As he finished climbing the ladder, the two men approached him with knives in their hands. "Let us see the necklace with the stone." After carefully observing it, they agreed it belonged to Wu-Pot'ki. They looked up at the tall Viking and asked, "Why do you come here?"

Thorvar then told them in detail what had happened, of Ne No, of the baby's death, and that he had come to avenge all these wrongdoings.

"Wu-Pot'ki said you should show me where this devil-man, Cherko, is hiding so I may find him and kill him."

The two men moved away to confer. Finally they turned back to Thorvar and the first one said, "We thought that this Cherko was hiding because, although he had done no wrong, someone evil was following him." The other one said, "Now that we know the true story, we would want to kill him also. Since Wu-Pot'ki has instructed us to show you where he is hiding, we will. Follow us."

They got down on their hands and knees and crawled through a long, low tunnel. As they emerged, Thorvar noticed that this cave and the cliff dwellings were not as large as those of Ne No's people, but much more secure. After a little more climbing, they reached the main floor.

Thorvar's appearance caused quite a commotion among the women and older children. But the two guards quickly assured them that no harm would come to them from this tall, strange looking man. They pointed out the room on the third level where Cherko was hiding.

The Viking planted his feet at the foot of the tall ladder to that room, and called out, "Cherko, I am Thorvar, mate of the woman Ne No. I have come to kill you for what you have done to my mate and to our baby, who died in her womb!"

When there was no reply Thorvar called again. "Come down here you woman stealer. Come down I say. I know you're there." Still no reply "If you don't come down, I'll come up and get you!"

Finally Cherko stuck his head out through the narrow door and whined, "I don't know what you're talking about. I had nothing to do with that. It must have been Ratum who did it. I wasn't even there!"

"Oh yes you were. Ne No recognized you." When nothing more was said, the Viking yelled, "Get ready Cherko. I'm coming up to get you!"

When Thorvar was a little over half way up the ladder, Cherko stuck his head out, grabbed the top of the ladder, and gave it a strong push backwards. As Thorvar and the ladder crashed to the hard floor below, the back of the Viking's head hit the top of a low rock wall. As he slumped to the floor, lifeless, the women and children, as well as the guards, backed farther away.

As soon as Cherko saw that Thorvar was lying there without movement, he gave a cry of glee. He climbed from one timber sticking out of the dwelling to another, over to a ladder at the room next to his. He hurried down with a look of triumph in his eyes. He stood astride his victim, glaring down on him. Then he kneeled down, and said in a loud voice, "Yes, I stole your wife while you were away. If it hadn't been for that clumsy one, Ratum, I'd have gotten away with her and had her for my woman. I'm glad she lost your baby in the fall!"

Then he wrapped his two hands around Thorvar's throat and as he tightened his grip, yelled, "Now, ugly big man, now I'll make sure that you are dead!" One of the guards stepped forward and Cherko pushed him aside with one hand. As he did so, Thorvar began to gasp for breath. Cherko then clamped both hands around his throat even tighter.

As the Viking struggled to breathe, he finally wrenched one of the Indian's hands from his throat and then, holding onto the wrist, rose with the full weight of his assailant still spread over his body. He struggled to get hold of Cherko's leg. Finally, he was able to grab his ankle and slowly rose to his feet.

Once up, he swung the Indian up over his head, still holding him by the one ankle and wrist. Cherko struggled, hitting the Viking in the face with his free hand, kicking with his free leg. The Viking, still holding him high over his head, walked slowly over to the three foot high balcony wall, and with a fierce yell of revenge, flung the Indian high over the wall, out and into the canyon far below.

As the screaming faded away and the echos diminished, all was suddenly hushed and still. And then in one great outburst, the women and guards crowded around Thorvar, cheering his triumph. Thorvar then sat down on the wall to clear his head of the dizziness from his fall. As he rested there, facing these strangers, he suddenly felt a great relief. The deep hurt that Ne No had suffered and the loss of her baby had been avenged. Later they could have another baby. He once more had peace of mind.

Some of the women continued to stand near him, chattering to each other. After a time, one of the guards came over to Thorvar and said, "The women are saying they are pleased you killed him. They are glad he is gone and will not molest them anymore when the men have gone to work on the temple. They would like you to rest here and when their men return from the temple this evening, have a meal with them.

Thorvar, although anxious to return to Ne No, recognized that this was their way of showing their thanks. He realized he must not offend them, and said, "Thank them for me. I will stay until the sun rises tomorrow."

The guards told him he was free to look around their cave. He replied, "Thank you. May I ask you some questions about your homes here?" They seemed delighted at his interest. "Does it get very cold living up here in the winter, since the sun shines into your cave only for a few hours in the morning each day?"

"Yes, when the afternoons and nights start getting colder, as the leaves change before they die and fall to the ground, we must cut much wood for our fires."

Thorvar replied, "You must need many fires to keep warm. This I can see as I look at the walls and ceiling near the back of your cave, covered with blackness."

"Again, it is so. But this cave is also one of the safest places to live," said the guard.

Thorvar nodded his head and said, "Yes, it is. It would be very hard for anyone to attack you. Is this the reason your people built up here?"

The guard smiled, "Yes, but there were other more important reasons why they built up here."

"More reasons? Such as what?"

The guard thought a minute. "Well, when our people lived on top of the mesa, other clans would steal their food when times were bad. Also, animals and snakes were a problem. Heavy rains and snows made the people wet and very uncomfortable.

"Occasionally, clans passing through would steal some of their women and small children. Now that we live up here in this cave, these things are not a problem."

Thorvar nodded, "I can see many reasons for your elders to make this move. But it must have been very hard getting all the things to build with up into this high cave."

"Yes. That is so. And some were killed falling into the canyon, trying to do this work. But it is good for us now."

When the sun was high overhead and they were in the shadows, the women fixed food for Thorvar. After he had eaten, he told them he needed to rest awhile, since his head was aching very badly from his fall.

The men returned late in the afternoon and when Wu-Pot'ki saw that Thorvar was still there, he was very pleased. Thorvar returned the necklace and thanked Wu-Pot'ki for his help.

After the meal, Thorvar was invited to sit around the campfire with them. They asked him many questions about places he had been. As they went to bed most of them agreed he was a good story teller, but that they all knew he was just making up stories to entertain them.

CHAPTER 20

W hen Thorvar awoke at sunrise, he noticed an Indian he had not seen before sitting near him with his legs crossed. As he rose from his mat, yawned, and stretched with his arms over his head, the little man got up and approached him.

Looking up, he said, "I listened to your story-telling last night and have heard of your killing the Devil Bird and the bad one called Cherko." He hesitated a moment and then continued, "Would you go with me to our cliff dwellings, not far from here? It is just across the next canyon."

Thorvar smiled and replied, "Why do you ask this?"

"We have many people there who would like to hear your story-telling around our campfire tonight. We have need of new stories such as yours. We have told the old stories so many times. Yours are different."

"But I have been gone for many days looking for the Devil Bird and visiting in the Valley of the Tall Ones. I need to return to my mate and tell her that she need fear Cherko no longer."

"Our cliff dwellings are on your way, and you could be back there early tomorrow after the sun rises."

Wu-Pot'ki, who overheard them talking, interrupted. "Thorvar, there are a great many of them living there, many more than live here. They are restless with the lack of rain for their crops and enough food to eat. They need new things to think and talk about, such as you tell. You could help them to forget, for a little while, their unrest."

Throvar rubbed the back of his head, which was still hurting from yesterday's fall, thought a bit and then said, "What is your name?"

"I am called Cho'na-ko. I am from the cliff dwellings where Cherko once lived, but was driven out because he was bad. Our people will want to see the great warrior who, while dazed and being choked by Cherko, rose up with him, held him high overhead, and with one mighty heave threw him into the canyon below."

The Viking pondered on this for awhile, then replied, "It was nothing. I was bigger. I did it only to avenge the pain he caused my mate and the death of our child."

Wu-Pot'ki encouraged him to go with Cho'na-ko for just the one day and evening, and after a little more prodding, he agreed. The Viking and Cho'na-ko followed the two guards through the long tunnel and watched them lower the long ladder. They climbed down, and as they were about to disappear around the cliff wall, the people above waved and gave a final yell of farewell.

They arrived at the top and walked northwest across the fairly level ground. As they approached the edge of Cho'na-ko's canyon, Thorvar saw the cliff dwelling where he lived. It faced southwest, as did Ne No's cave opening, so they would have plenty of sunshine and warmth in winter. As they approached the cave, he was surprised to see how very large it was, and how high up in the cliff (Cliff Palace, at Mesa Verde). It appeared to contain at least twice as many dwellings, a great many more kivas, and a much larger number of people than their dwelling by the spruce trees. There was a much steeper slope down the face of the cave and trash was strewn all around.

Again, as happened everywhere Thorvar went, the people stared at the "odd looking man," walking with Cho'na-ko. The two of them went down into one of the many kivas. Cho'na-ko went to talk to the men who had gathered off to the side, while Thorvar waited at the bottom of the ladder. As he waited, he noticed one man, who seemed to be arguing with the other. He was broad shouldered with a big chest, and it seemed as if he had no neck because his head was set down into his shoulders. His large body was supported by thin, scrawny legs.

After a time, several of them came over with Cho'na-ko. The one with no neck, who swaggered as if he were someone of importance, cleared his throat and said arrogantly, "Cho'na-ko has been telling us about you. I have decided to let you stay here today and sit with us around our campfire this evening. But you will only sit and listen." And with that, he turned away, as if dismissing this "intruder."

Thorvar turned to Cho'na-ko and said, "You know this was not my idea in the first place. I think I'll leave now and return to my own dwellings." He climbed the ladder and started to leave.

Cho'na-ko and most of the others quickly followed him up the ladder and hurried after him. "Please stay and visit with us the rest of the day and evening," pleaded several of them.

"Why should I stay? It is certain from the way your `important one' spoke that I am not really welcome here. I will go." He started to leave.

They pursued him saying, "It is the desire of all of us, except him, that you stay and tell your stories as you did last night at Wu-Pot'ki's dwellings. He thinks you will become more important than he is in the eyes of our people if they hear of your conquests. We will handle him."

The Viking shrugged his shoulder and replied, "I will stay only if he comes to me in front of his people, and in a convincing manner ask me to stay and talk at your campfire, I would much rather leave, but I am trying to do what Wu-Pot'ki and Cho'na-ko asked me to do."

They went back down into the kiva and, after a time, emerged with the "important one." With a glare of poorly veiled hatred in his eyes, he nevertheless choked out, "I would be honored if you would stay the day with us and tell your stories around our campfires this evening."

Thorvar accepted coldly, knowing that he now had one more enemy to watch.

Cho'na-ko and several others spent the rest of the day escorting him around their large cave and many dwellings. Thorvar noted the same care and good workmanship in their construction as he had seen in the other dwellings.

Thorvar asked, "How many kivas do you have here? It appears that you have three times as many as we have."

One of them replied, "Yes, that is right. We have many clans and people living here."

He asked them where they got water for so many people.

Cho'na-ko replied, "That is one of our problems, especially now, since we have not had much rain and there is little water from the winter's snow. We must go down across the canyon below the rain god temple (Sun Temple, Mesa Verde) for water for our people. We have hardly any water nearby, and must depend on catching rain and snow melt water in large clay pots or woven baskets. When our 'old ones' were building their dwellings in this cave there were several large springs below with plenty of water. But they are all about dried up now. So we have to go a greater distance, especially in the past several years.."

As Thorvar looked and climbed around these crowded dwellings, he was impressed by the tall buildings as well as with the cleverness with which so many of the lower dwellings fit so closely together. He thought to himself that he was glad Ne No did not live here. There were far too many people. They would have no privacy at all.

At the evening meal, which was sparse for all, he notice he had been given a double helping of everything. Thorvar looked around and saw several children leaning against a wall, gulping down their meager helpings of food. They looked so thin and hungry. He got up, went to where they sat, and put all of his food in their little pottery bowls. They looked up at him with their big, sad eyes, as he sat down beside them.

He was particularly attracted to one of them, a boy of good size, but very thin, who seemed sad and lonely. When the youth had gobbled up his food and saw Thorvar looking at him, he came over and sat down nearby. After a time, he move a little closer. Finally, after some hesitation, he moved over and sat up close beside this strange looking man. Thorvar smiled at him, put his arm around his shoulder and they sat there quietly, content to be together.

As night began to close in, the big fire in the area where they had been eating was replenished with wood, and as it blazed high, Cho'na-ko called for the people to gather. He called to the Viking to come over where he stood, and then in a loud voice said that this very large man with the pale skin and burned hair had come from a far-away place to live in the nearby cliff dwellings of Nakota, Tonato, and Nonacho.

As Thorvar stood beside him, Cho'na-ko put his hand up on the Viking's shoulder and proclaimed loudly, "His name is Thorvar. This mighty warrior, since the last full moon, sought out and killed the Devil Bird in the Shining Mountains. Yesterday he avenged his mate's injuries and the death of the baby she was carrying within her. That was caused by Cherko, the bad one we drove out of our cliff dwellings some time ago.

As the people cheered loudly, they began crowding around the big fire. When there was no more room, more climbed up on the roofs of nearby dwellings.

"He has rid us of two of our worst enemies. We have asked him to come here and tell us of strange places he has been and strange things he has seen far away from here."

As the evening wore on, Thorvar was asked and answered many questions late into the night.

The next morning, when Thorvar awakened, he was surprised to feel someone snuggled beside him. He opened his eyes and saw the boy whom he sat with the day before. He stood up quietly, to avoid disturbing the boy's sleep. Cho'na-ko, who was lying nearby, smiled and said, "He likes you. He has no father or mother, they are both dead. He lives with his mother's mother and their clan. He misses his father."

After the two men had eaten together, Thorvar prepared to return to Ne No and her people. Cho'na-ko thanked him for staying and telling his stories to the people. "They are already busy talking and arguing about the many new things you told them. It will get their minds off the lack of rain and food for awhile."

The Viking bid goodby to several of the men when suddenly the boy appeared and begged Thorvar to take him too. Soon the Mother of his clan came and took him gently by the hand and walked away. Thorvar waved at him as he departed. He climbed up to the level ground above, and with big strides, hurried home to Ne No.

CHAPTER 21

When Thorvar started his descent from the plateau to their own cliff dwellings, he reminded himself once again to use the correct hand and toe holes. As he came walking down the cliff ledge toward the cave, he was startled by someone yelling at the top of his voice, "There's Thorvar! He is back!" With that "announcement" Natcha came running to the Viking and flung his arms around the big man. Thorvar patted the boy on the back and they walked down together as Ne No came hurrying to his side.

He put his arms around her as she buried her head in his chest. With tears of relief she said, "Oh, Toe-War, I am so glad you are home. Are you alright?"

"Yes Ne No, I am fine. And you need not fear Cherko any more."

The boy interrupted, "Did you kill him, Thorvar? Did you?"

"Yes, I got rid of him. Now, I want to be alone with Ne No for the rest of the day."

This was not to be, since some of the people had heard what he told Ne No and Natcha, and they all came asking questions.

It was some time before he and Ne No could slip away, down the path into the canyon to their special, secluded place near the spring. There, Ne No asked him to tell her what had happened during the last few days.

He told her and then asked about the tall boy, Natcha. "Oh, Toe-war, his father will not have anything to do with him. He says he cannot be his child, since he is so tall, and so his mother agrees that the boy could not possibly be their son."

Thorvar shook his head saying, "I'll go talk to them and explain how he became so tall." They walked, hand in hand, up the path to the dwellings.

When Thorvar returned from talking to them he shook his head sadly as he told his mate, "You are right. They absolutely refuse to accept him as their son."

Just then Natcha came walking slowly to where they were seated. "Thorvar, since they don't think I am their son, and I don't remember them either, can I be your son? I want to be your son and live with you and Ne No?"

"Well Natcha, we will think about it. And for tonight you can eat and sleep in our dwelling with us."

Later, when Natcha was not around, Ne No told Thorvar, "I think it would be wonderful to have him for our son. You enjoy being together and you could teach him many things. I have grown very fond of him with his manly and kind young ways."

"Well, since I know you mean what you say, I will talk to the man and his mate once more tomorrow, to explain again why he is so tall, and see if they will accept him as their son."

The next morning, the man and woman again refused to accept Natcha. Thorvar than called for a member from each clan to meet in the largest kiva and explain this to them. After a short discussion, they all agreed that Natcha should, hereafter, be recognized as the son of Thorvar and Ne No.

When Natcha was told of the decision, he jumped up and down with happiness and Ne No said, "Toe-war, now you and I have a fine son after all."

The next morning, after the three of them had eaten, the Viking looked over at the tall boy. "Come with me, son. If you are going to be my son, I want to teach you how to fight and defend yourself as all good Vikings do." Natcha followed eagerly as they climbed the cliff, following Thorvar's instructions concerning the climbing holes. On top, they found a clear space, away from the crops, for the lesson of attack and defense.

After a time, they sat down to rest. Natcha, sitting close to the Viking, looked at him and said, "Thorvar, when we were back in the cave of the tall people you told their two Chiefs that you had come from a far away land, across a great body of water."

"Yes, I remember."

"Well, was that just a story you told them, or did you really come from such a far away place?"

"Yes, I come from far across a great body of water. As time goes by, on certain evenings I will tell you and Ne No more about my home, things I have not told before. I will tell each of you much more because I hope to return with you and Ne No to my homeland. But first, I need to find the large body of water I must cross."

As they sat there talking, they noticed someone running from the cliff edge toward them. When he came closer, they realized it was Tanoto. After catching his breath he said, "Thorvar! A messenger from Wu-Pot'ki has just arrived He wants to talk to our leaders and he wants you to be there too. I seemes to be important."

They all descended to the dwellings and were told that Tanoto and Thorvar should go down into their largest kiva where others had gathered They were surprised to see that several of the other clan Mothers were presen - a very, very unusual occurrence.

As soon as they had arrived the messenger said, "Wu-Pot'ki and members of several other large cliff dwellings request that you send three representatives to the temple we are building. He is asking that all other clif dwellings send their leaders too.

"It is not to continue our work on the temple, but to hold a meeting of great importance to all of us. They have suggested that you send Tanoto, Nakota, and Thorvar tomorrow morning to represent you."

Tanoto asked, "For what purpose is this large meeting?"

"It is about the drought, which is becoming of increasing concern to all of us."

In the morning the three of them went to the temple. Representatives from all the large cliff dwelling at Mesa Verde had gathered in the area inside the walls.

Wu-Pot'ki then climbed up on the wall of the large circular structure they were building and said, "I am sure that most of your people, like ours, are becoming quite concerned about the lack of rain. Many years ago we had plenty of food, we had buffalo, sheep with big horns, and deer. Now they are moving farther and farther away from us. Now we must eat the smaller animals, rabbits, squirrels, and turkeys. It takes many more of these small ones and much more hunting to feed our growing number of people.

"For many years, as stories have been heard around our campfires, one that was often told by our ancestors and repeated down through the many generations is this one. Some five days travel from here, toward the setting sun and warmer country, many people lived in three narrow, high-walled canyons, where there is a river flowing with much water (Canyon de Chelly, Arizona).

"The story is that there was so much water in this river, that the people who lived beside it were forced to build their dwellings up in the sheer cliffs. This was because their shelters down by the river were being washed away. We do not know if this place still has so much water, but some of us think it would be wise to consider going there."

This caused quite a bit of confusion and loud talk. Some thought it should be done. Others did not think it wise to leave the security they now had just because of some old tales they had heard.

Tanoto got up on the wall beside Wu-Pot'ki, got the attention of the group, and said, loudly, "I suggest that we talk among ourselves and consider this."

Later in the afternoon they gathered together again. It was decided to have a small group of volunteers make the trip to determine if such a place existed, how much water was there.

Wu-Pot'ki asked for volunteers. Eight of them including Nakota and Tanoto, offered to go. Then one of the volunteers got up on the wall and called, "Thorvar! Will you go with us? You would be welcome and would serve as extra protection for our group."

Thorvar was silent for a moment, but as encouragement swelled from the crowd, he yelled out, "If you want me, I will go!" And so it was decided.

Wu-Pot'ki quieted those present. "I am very pleased that we have been building this temple to the rain gods because it also serve as a place to meet and discuss things, such as this, that concern all of us. For those of you who have come some distance, remember that the many small rooms we are building on the inside of the main walls can be used for places for you to stay tonight."

As they started to disband, he called for their attention one more time. "You volunteers, and others who might decide to go on this trip, should meet at Tanoto and Nakota's cliff dwellings two days from today when the sun is high. Bring your food, water and weapons."

When the three of them returned to their dwellings that evening, Tanoto called their people together and told them of what had occured at the meeting.

Later, when Ne No, Thorvar, and Natcha went into their dwelling, Ne No nestled down on her big man's lap and quietly said, "Since you are going on this trip, Toe-war, I am going with you."

Natcha quickly interrupted with, "Me too."

Thorvar looked at both of them, very surprised by Ne No's comments. "But it will be a hot, hard journey, and I will not be gone long."

"I don't care," replied Ne No. "I am going with you this time."

"But why, Ne No?"

"Because one of these time I am afraid you may not return. Wherever you go, I want to go too."

They discussed this into the night, and at Ne No's insistance, it was finally decided that she and Natcha would go.

The next morning, when the word circulated that Ne No was going, Tanoto's mate, and Nonacho and his mate decided they wanted to be included.

CHAPTER 22

F or the rest of the day, those who were going on this trip, a group that now included eight people just from their cliff dwelling were busy making more sandals and water bags, checking their bows and arrows, gathering food, and other things they would need.

Since early summer was now upon them, the women were making things to cover their heads to protect them from the sun. They were aided by other women so they would be sure to be ready when the time came to leave.

There was a feeling of excitement among these volunteers. They thought about finding a new place to live where there might be plenty of water.

However, many of the women, as they assisted those about to depart, were not so sure they liked the idea of having to leave their homes. They were so secure here. It was a dry and warm place where they lived. Surely the rains would come again soon and there would be plenty of food. Besides, what dangers might befall them in a far-away place?

Toward noon of the next day, six representatives of the other cliff dwellings arrived. They were quite put out that women were going with them. This was no trip for women. They would slow them down. In case of attack, the men would have to fight to keep them from being taken away. Those things concerned them.

But when the sun was high in the sky, this group of fourteen people, three of whom were women and one a tall boy, went down into the canyon and started their journey toward the open plains below.

As they traveled southwest, the thin ground cover of prairie grass was still green. The dark green bushes and small, pinon pines covered parts of the scattered waves of sandy soil. It was mostly flat country with sagebrush, yucca, and open space that reached to the horizon.

Toward evening they settled down on a ridge beside some small pinon pines that would give some protection from the wind. As the women spread their mats, several of the men gathered brush and made a fire to keep them warm.

The next morning, after eating sparingly of their provisions, they were off again on their southwest trek, in good spirits. In the early part of the morning they came across a small creek bed, but it was almost dry. As they continued on, they noticed that the prairie grass and bushes on the sandy ridges were becoming more sparse. Off in the distance they saw several long mesas similar to theirs.

Toward dusk they approached another slightly larger creek bed, but it was dry too. Each time they had hoped to find a supply of water that might benefit their people, but each time they were disappointed.

They were tempted to spend the night in the creek bed, protected and out of sight. But Tanoto reminded them that sometimes the black clouds could appear suddenly rain very hard for a short time, and a wall of water would rush down through the arroyo, sweeping all before it. Nakota replied, "Well, if we could bring rain to all of us in this manner, I say let's sleep down here tonight and maybe we can tempt our rain gods." The others agreed, and so they did.

The next morning they rose with mixed emotions when nothing had happened. They began walking in the early morning freshness. Ne No noticed Thorvar studying the landscape ahead of them. He ran over to a high ridge, climbed to the top, and with his hands cupped over his eyes, peered into the distance. Soon he came running down the ridge yelling with joy. He ran up to Ne No and excitedly said, "Ne No! I see a ship with large sails off in the distance. It would be a ship of the size that sail on a very, very large body of water, which I have told about. This is just what I have been trying to find for so long. It may be a ship that can take us back to my homeland!"

Nakota overheard him and said, "This cannot be, Thorvar, We are in a desert land. We would have heard from travelers if such a body of water was only several days away from us."

But Thorvar, in his excitement, was not to be reasoned with. "No Nakota! It is a sail ship. Sure it is still some distance away, but it is a ship." He grabbed Ne No and Natcha's hands and hurried off.

As they disappeared into the distance, Tanoto and Nakota shook their heads and the latter said, "He is going to be so disappointed. I do not think there is any large body of water there. As I told him, if there were, we would have been told of it."

Tanoto replied, "I am also certain it does not exist, but he seemed so sure. Well, at least they are going in the same direction that we must go."

As the group followed Thorvar's footsteps in the sandy soil, they began to see what Thorvar had been so excited about and as they drew somewhat nearer, they could see a group of sizeable rock formations piercing the horizon, with one very tall one seeming to point to the sky above. (Shiprock, New Mexico) Late in the day, as they approached these formations, they saw Thorvar and Ne No and the boy, all sitting at the base of the tallest one. It rose well over one thousand feet straight up from the surrounding ground level.

Thorvar rose and came to meet them. In a very dejected voice he said quietly, "I was so sure it was a sea-going ship. The nearer I got, the more I thought it was. Then when I began to wonder if it might just be a very tall rock formation, I would suddenly see blue water ahead of me spread out over the horizon. As we hurried on, it seemed to surround my ship. then as we approached much near, the water was gone (a mirage) and I realized it was only a very tall rock formation."

As Nakota and Tanoto and several others sat down on large boulders a short distance from the formation, the Viking pointed saying, "See how the top of this formation tapers up to two peaks?" Well, that is what looked like large sails from a distance. And the lower part of it seemed to extend out like the hull of the ship."

His friends both looked at him enquiringly and Nakota asked "My friend, what do you mean by 'sails'? And what are they used for?'

"Well, sails are very large, heavy pieces of cloth, spread out on masts, like tall poles, attached to the deck of the ship. When the wind blows, it pushes against the sails and makes the ship move through the water." Nakota, Tanoto, and others nodded their heads, obviously not having the vaguest idea of what he was talking about.

The Viking stooped to one knee looking directly at his friends, "Why did I see lots of blue water at times and then when I got there, it was gone?"

They had no answer. One said, "It just happens at times in this bare, hot countryside. Some think it is the gods playing tricks on us."

As they all settled down for the night at the base of these large rock formations in this wide-open wasteland, Ne No saw that her mate was very quiet. She snuggled up to him and whispered, "Tow-war. I am very sorry it was not your - what you call it - ship, but together we will find whatever it is you are looking for, I am sure." He gave her a kiss and gradually slipped off to sleep.

For the next three days and nights nothing unusual happened They were becoming weary from walking over the hot sand with the sun beating down on them. Also, they were getting short of water and food.

When they arose on the seventh day of their trip, they were obviously tired. After they ate, one of them made the comment that soon they would have to start supplementing their remaining food with food off the land. In the late afternoon, several of the men who had gone ahead of the main group, came hurrying back. One of them exclaimed, "Up ahead, in the distance, we can see what we think is an enormous, wide hole in the ground." They began to move a little faster until they, too, could see it. As they approached, several people noticed that it seemed to spread out in three directions. Several others began to get excited saying. "This may be the place we have been seeking."

Reaching the rim of this great opening, they were awed as they looked down into a deep, long canyon. They saw its flat, sandy bottom many, many hundreds of feet below. It extended for a great distance in both directions. Tanoto cried, out, "Look! I see a very narrow stream of water flowing along the canyon floor. There is water!" (Canyon de Chelly - Arizona)

They sat on the rim, looking at the beauty of the sheer walls and the red sandstone formations in the canyon. As they looked, they saw a number of dwellings near the stream. Because the canyon was so deep, the people moving around below looked very small.

The men began talking about how to get down into its depths. They were suddenly interrupted by Natcha, "Here is a way down! Come look! It is a path!"

There was a path that looked very steep and treacherous, especially for the three women. While a few of the men began mumbling again about having women along, Ne No and Natcha started down the steep and narrow path. Quickly, Thorvar followed and then the other two women grabbed their mate's hands and began their descent. The other followed quietly.

It was slow going and required much attention to not slip and fall on the pebbly, sandy surface of the trail. It wound down among rocks and bushes for about five hundred feet and at one place crossed a creek. At that point, they stopped to get a drink and rest for a short time. Then they continued downward and finally arrived on the canyon floor.

They were greeted by a number of curious children who had been watching their descent and then by several men, who seemed friendly. Nakota began by saying, "It is a very steep climb down from the top. Are there other ways we might have come?"

One the natives, after some hesitation, said, "Yes, there are other ways. Why do you come?"

Tanota stepped forward and said, "We come from many cliff dwellings back toward the rising sun. We come seeking a place to live where our people can have water to grow crops and food to eat. We seem to have less rain each passing year and our crops and food are becoming less and less.

The Indian stood silent, quietly listening to Tanoto's words. Tanoto continued, "We have been walking these many days to find you, since we have heard from our 'old ones' that you have much water."

The native nodded his head. "Yes, for many years we had much water from our river and rains. But now, for some years, we have had less and less water, as you can see from the small amount of water flowing in the big river bed over there. We are also worried about having enough crops to feed all our people. Many have left to hunt places of rain and water, just as you are doing." He continued, "Yes, as you see, we do still have some water in our river, but not enough. We might be able to have a few of your people come live with us, but not many. You are welcome to spend a few days and nights with us while you rest. Maybe around our campfire we can share new stories with your people."

Tanoto and Nakota thanked him for his friendliness and offer, saying, "This is good of you. Our women are tired and we all need rest tonight. But tomorrow night we would enjoy sitting around your fire to hear and tell old and new stories with all of you."

Their people then showed them a place where they could have their own privacy near the stream and where water would be convenient for them. Soon several women brought food for them. As the women walked away, they turned and looked back at Throvar, Ne No heard one of them say to the other, "Isn't that big one there strange looking?"

As they settled down for the night in this deep, well protected canyon, there was a general feeling of comfort and security, in contrast to the way they felt living on the hot, desolate land the past seven days.

They were awakened the next morning by the sun shining down the length of the canyon where they had slept. With the sun light in the canyon they were able to really look around and see things. As Thorvar and Ne No stood looking at the varying colors in the sandstone wall of the canyon, they felt as if they might fall over backwards as their gaze proceeded up the great height of the sheer walls.

Nonacho called to his sister, "Ne No! Look at the rock dwellings in the cave up there (White House, Canyon de Chelly).

Ne No replied, "Yes, I see them. See how they are well protected far back under the cliff, which leans outward above them?" Their gaze dropped to dwellings below this cave on the canyon floor, near the river. They noticed that some of these dwellings were built like their ancestors of sandstone blocks on slightly elevated ground.

Then their attention was diverted by three men coming from this village toward them. As they approached, they appeared to be Elders of their village and did not seem as friendly as those who had greeted them the evening before.

CHAPTER 23

Back at the cliff dwellings, Ne No's mother and several other women were checking their dwindling supply of beans, corn, and squash, which were kept in a small storage room built against the side of the cliff. They removed enough food for the day's meals and carefully closed the opening to the storge room, sealing off even the smallest openings. This was necessary to keep the rats, mice and chipmucks from eating their diminishing provisions.

Ne No's mother sat down with a small woven bag of violet striped beans beside her, put the corn on the slightly concaved slab of rock and was beginning to grind it, when she noticed a very tall man coming up the path from the canyon. He was so tall that as he came nearer, she started to get up to go into her dwelling. However, he called to her in a pleasant manner, so she remained where she was sitting.

He said, "I look for Thorvar. I'm his friend."

"He is not here now."

"Where is he? I come from far away to see him. He is an old friend."

Most of the men were up above in the fields. But one of the older men was sitting farther over in the cave. She pointed to him.

"Go talk to him." She then went into her dwelling.

The tall one went over and called up to the old one, "I'm looking for my friend. Thorvar. Where is he?"

"He is not here. He is gone."

"Where?"

"To a place where the `old ones' told us, long ago, there is plenty of water."

"Where is it?"

"Toward the setting sun and down where it is warm."

"How long ago?"

"Two suns ago."

Ne No's mother looked out of her dwelling, and as she saw the tall one going down the path into the canyon, she noticed a sizeable sore on his back which had healed only recently. She wondered how he had hurt himself. As she sat down to resume her grinding, she could not find her small bag of beans. She looked all around her. It was gone.

After walking down the canyon for some time, Wa-Gu-er'o emerged onto the plateau. He was thankful he had gotten a good drink and filled his tightly woven bag with water from their pool at the foot of the trail before going up to seek the pale one. Now he sat down to eat a few beans from the small woven bag. He was very disappointed that his vowed enemy was not there. But he would follow the footprints that he had so easily found. He smiled as he thought of Thorvar and his friend, and how easy they would be to trail, as long as a wind storm did not blow the footprints away. The tracks had helped him so far, he hoped they would continue.

His friend, Wa-Sho, has stayed with him while his back was healing. But he would not come with him. He went with the other of the Wa tribe when they left for a new place to live. As he thought about these things, he encouraged himself by saying aloud, "I don't need him anyway. I want the pleasure of killing this Thorvar all by myself. I will make him pay for what he did to me."

He moved relentlessly forward and fortunately, for him, the wind did not blow nor did it rain to disturb the many footprints. As some days went by, he began to eat and drink only when really necessary. He thought how fortunate he was that he had refilled his water bag and taken the bag of beans. He said aloud to himself, "In the mountains where I was raised, food was plentiful in the valley. But here on this hot, wide open space, there is nothing to eat, and very little water."

CHAPTER 24

T he three Elders, looking rather unfriendly, approached. One said, "We wish to speak with your leaders. Where can we find them?"

Nonacho pointed at Tanoto and Nakota who were standing together looking off in the distance at a very tall red sandstone formation rising from the canyon floor, admiring its stark beauty.

As they approached the two of them, one of the Elders said, "You and your people are most welcome to spend some days and nights with us while you rest. However, there is one in your group who concerns our people. He is that large, strange looking one standing over there. Will you go with us while we talk to him?"

They nodded their heads in agreement, but Tanoto inquired, "Yes, but why do you wish to talk to him?"

"Well, one of our women, after bringing your food last night, told others of this strange looking man. They are worried because of him."

Nakota called to Thorvar, who came over to join them. The spokesman from the village looked up at the tall Viking and then spoke in a friendly manner, "Our people are concerned about you. Although you are big and seem strong and walk easily, they wonder if you have a sickness."

Thorvar smiled and replied, "Why would they think that I am sick? I am very well and strong as you can see." He went over and picked up a very large, heavy boulder, and with little effort, heaved it aside.

It was apparent that the three of them were impressed but the spokesman continued, "They think you are sick because your skin is so pale, as if you are dying. Your hair is the color of dead weeds. Your eyes have changed color - they are a cold blue like some of the rocks from which we make our necklaces. They wish you to leave so you will not die here. They feel it might leave a curse on them."

At this point, Nakota stepped forward and said, "This man is not sick. He is very strong and well. He has lived among all of our people for most of two summers and a winter. He has always looked like this since the day he came to live with us."

"Then why does he look so sick? Why does he look like he is dying? We have never seen one like this before."

Tanoto interrupted, "He looks different from all of us because he come from a land far away, across a great body of water. In his land, all look like him. It is a great land."

"That is hard to believe. Our Ancient Ones have never told us of such a land or people."

"No, and we had never been told of such places or people. But we are all convinced that such people and place do exist. He does not lie, he always speaks truth."

Nakota intervened, "He has caused no curse to come upon us. He is a brave man who has helped defend our people against our enemies. He is mated to our lovely woman, Ne No, whom you see visiting with some of your children. Does she look as if a curse has befallen her?"

The three Elders moved off to the side, obviously arguing among themselves. After a time they returned and, facing Throvar, said, "We are now satisfied that you are not sick - just different. But in order to convince our people, will you tell all of us tonight around our big fire about yourself and from where you come?"

Thorvar smiled, "Yes, I will talk to you. But will you tell your people that what I will say is the truth? It is not just a story. So many people think I am making up stories just to entertain them. Some even call me 'The Great Story-Teller.'"

The three said they would go back to their people and tell them he was not sick. They would also tell them he would explain it all that evening around their fire.

During the rest of the day, they enjoyed looking around this enchanting and fertile canyon. They were a bit envious when they saw the crops being grown right on the canyon floor, where it was convenient for them to work on their crops and guard them from birds and small animals. The soil seemed to be very arable, Tanoto throught, as he picked some of it up in his hand. This was so different from their way of living, where they had to climb up the cliff side to plant, work, and guard the crops above their dwellings. And during the dry times, they also had to carry water up to their crops.

Several of those who had greeted them the day before came over to visit. Tanoto said "We have been observing how fortunate you are to have a river so near and such good ground to grow crops."

"Yes, but our ancestors were often driven out when their homes washed away. Heavy rains still flood parts of this canyon. This is why they finally had to build up in the cliff, just as you see those stone dwellings up there."

Nakota enquired, "From above, when we looked down into this canyon, it appeared to go a great distance in both directions."

"Yes. There are two other large and long canyons like this which meet ours toward the setting sun. There are people living there, many of whom now live up in the cliff dwellings.

As they walked over to the cliff, Nakota noted some paintings on the wall. Their guide said, "Yes, on the walls of all three of these canyons there are pictures of people, animals, and sometimes designs."

Ne No wanted to show Natcha some of these paintings, but could not find him. She called out his name. When she received no reply, Thorvar tried. Soon they heard the boy answering their calls but they couldn't see him. As they looked around, he yelled. "Here I am, up here!" They saw him in the cave dwellings up on the side of the cliff.

Thorvar called back, "That's alright. We just wanted to know where you were." Then he and Ne No went down by the river and sat under some trees - just resting enjoying each other's company.

Evening arrived and the big fire was lit. Some of the people still avoided Thorvar. However, by the time he had talked about his people and his homeland, the people crowded around him asking many questions.

Nakota took his turn telling how his friend helped them fight the vicious northern Indians and kill the big bird they called Devil Bird. When the tales were told, and as the people started toward their dwellings, many talked enthusiastically about the big man, his "stories," and his strenght as a great warrior.

The next evening they all gathered again around the big fire. Two travelers who had come in from the west were welcomed also.

As the evening stories were about to begin, one of the Elders rose and said, "Last evening around our fire, two of our guests, known as Thorvar and Nakota, told us great stories. Tonight we have two new visitors. We would like to invite them to come closer to our fire and tell us of their home and things they have seen."

And so the two of them came forward and the one said, "I am Kiowa, this is my companion Cuerno. You have greeted us as friends today. We thank you for your food and friendliness. We were here once before when we were younger. My friend and I enjoy traveling and seeing things. We wanted to visit your canyon once more, since it is beautiful and safe, with good water and good crops.

"You ask us to tell of our home. We live in a small village in part of a canyon that is even bigger and more beautiful then yours (the Grand Canyon). There is a very swift river running through it that always carries a great amount of water (the Colorado River) Some, who have visited our village and have come from the land of the setting sun, say the water from this great river flows into a very large body of water that reaches as far as the eyes can see. They say this body of water is a great many days' journey from our home."

With these last comments, Thorvar rose up and in an excited voice interrupted, "Did they say whether this great body of water had large waves of water that surged up onto the land and then flowed back where they came from?"

The speaker looked surprised, not only at the question but, at the appearance of the man who asked it. After some hesitation, he replied, "No. They did not tell us anything like that."

"Did they say whether the water had a salty taste to it?" Again, looking a little puzzled, the speaker replied, "No. They did not say."

"How far away toward the setting sun is your village and this great river?"

Kiowa smiled and said, "The travel takes the time from when the moon is dark until it is half a moon. Why do you ask? Would you like to come visit us some time in our village? You would be welcome."

The Elder who had invited Kiowa to talk interrupted saying, "Thorvar, let the man, Kiowa, continue with his stories."

Thorvar bowed his head, "I am sorry. I will not interrupt again."

As soon as the gathering was over, he sought out Kiowa and Cuerno. "I know I look different from all of you. Most people in my land have the same light skin, the same hair and eyes. I come from a land far across a very large body of water such as you were talking about this evening. I've been searching for a long time for this large body of water to cross and return to my homeland."

Kiowa looked up at him questioningly, "How could you possibly cross such a great body of water? No one could possibly swim that far."

"I know it sounds impossible. Three seasons ago I really did cross such a great body of water in what we call a `ship'."

"What is a ship?"

"I will tell you more about this later. Now I need to know, do you think your river goes to such a large body of water, far beyond your village?"

"We think so. The visitors who told us even showed us shells that they picked up beside the water. Our women thought they were pretty and got us to trade food to them for many of the shells."

Now the Viking became even more interested. "Do you have any of those shells with you?"

"Yes. Here are some of them."

Thorvar held some of them in his hand. "I have seen many such shells along our shore. Are you both returning to your village before long?"

"Yes, we are going to rest for another sundown and after getting fresh water here and trading for food, we are going to start back to our village."

Thorvar was becoming quite excited. He looked down at Kiowa and asked, "Did you really mean it earlier this evening when you said I could come visit you in your village?"

"Yes, I meant it. You and any others who would like to may come back with us when we leave. Keep in mind that it is a long, hot journey to our beautiful canyon and village. You will have to bring your own food and water. There are springs where we can find water, especially this early in the summer, when we have occasional rains across the prairie. But when our food is gone, we will have to eat what we can hunt and find."

"I wish to go with you. My mate and son must also go with me."

Kiowa and Guerno both shook their heads. "It would be a very long and hard trip for them. It would not be wise."

"Nevertheless, I wish to have them go with us."

"It is your family, but we want you to know what they will face."

"It is done then. We will all three go with you the second sunrise from now." Thorvar hurried to their resting place and told Ne No of what he had arranged.

All Ne No said was, "Where you go, I go also."

When Natcha heard this he blurted out, "I want to go too. Can I Thorvar?"

Thorvar replied, "Son, where Ne No and I go, you will go. But I want both of you to know that this will be a much longer and more tiring trip than the one we just completed. We could die in this desert land."

The next morning, when the others heard that Thorvar and his family were leaving, there was much commotion.

Nakota said to Thorvar, "Friend, I will go with you."

When Nonacho learned that his sister was going, he decided that he and his mate were going too.

Thorvar hurried over to where Kiowa and Cuerno were resting to tell them. Kiowa looked somewhat concerned. "Well, it is up to them if they all want to go. I think that Cuerno and I should meet with all of them and tell them of the dangers, it will be a long and very rough trip. We might run into bad sandstorms and we might run out of food for so many. It can also be hard for some of the men."

Despite the warning, everyone except Tanoto and his mate decided to go.

Late that night, Tanoto met Thorvar by the river bank. The Viking was pacing back and forth unable to sleep because he was so excited.

As he approached he said, "Thorvar, we have decided to go. We started on this trip to see if we could find water and a new place for many of our people to live. Although it seems as if some of our people could move here, since there is a small stream, according to Kiowa there is a great amount of water in that river. There would not be enough water here for many of our people."

At the first light of dawn they were getting ready for the trip. They filled their water bags and rolled up their mats while Kiowa, Cuerno, and Thorvar went to the village Elders to ask for food for their trip. The Elders readily traded food for the pretty and unusual ornamental shells they offered. However, when Thorvar had nothing to give, they denied his request.

As Thorvar dejectedly started to turn away, he decided to make one more effort. "If you will give me just enough food for the eight of us, I will promise you that if we find the river with plenty of water, which Kiowa spoke of, I will get the word back to you."

The Elders didn't budge. "How do we know that you will do this?"

"You have heard my friends say that I always tell the truth, I always keep my word. And you have said that your water supply has been diminishing, and that some of your people have already left, looking for a new place to live."

The three Elders walked to the side to talk to each other. Finally, they returned to the big man and said, "Thorvar, We believe you speak the truth. It is true that we are searching for a place with more water for our people. We will give you the food your eight people need but forget about returning to tell us of the water."

With great joy he hurried back to his own people to tell them the news. When he arrived, he saw the six representatives from the other cliff dwellings, who had traveled with them, waiting for him. Several of them asked, "What will we tell our people when the six of us return to our cliff dwellings without you?"

Thorvar replied, "Tell our people and yours that there is not enough water here now for all of them to come live. Tell them that our people are going to see a place where we have heard there is much water. They nodded their heads and said, "This is true. We will tell them."

By late morning, each of them had received a generous portion of food from their hosts. After checking to make sure they had their weapons as well as their water and food, they picked up the women's sleeping mats and turned toward the west to begin their journey.

Just as Thorvar turned, he was suddenly confronted by a seven-foot tall Indian, standing with his arms spread far apart.

"I found you. I will kill you now!" And with that, he lunged at Thorvar with his knife. Everyone scattered.

The Viking, although surprised, managed to step quickly aside, avoiding the rush. While the tall Indian was recovering his balance, Thorvar threw Ne No's bed mat, as well as the other things he was carrying, off to the side, He did not have time to get his knife out of his food bag.

The Indian sneered as he realized that the pale faced one had no knife.

The tall boy, Natcha ran up to the Indian and yelled, " Wa-Gu-er'o! Thorvar could not help hurting you when you sneaked up and jumped on his back! You were choking him to death!"

Wa-Gu-er'o knocked the boy to the ground with a vicious back hand to the face. This unnecessary roughness to the boy caused the confident smile on Thorvar's face to change to a determined scowl.

The people saw that some excitement was developing and came rushing up to watch, although they stayed at a safe distance. It was a most unusual setting, a crowd of short, dark-skinned Indians of the plains, watching two much taller men. One was a white-skinned man from a far-away land. He was well proportioned and very strong. His adversary was an Indian from the mountains, also well proportioned, who stood at least a head taller than the Viking. His power was obviously in his muscular strength plus his greater height and longer arms.

As the Indian moved deliberately toward the Viking, holding his knife out in front of him, he yelled, "Now I kill!"

Thorvar swiftly stepped forward, grabbed his wrist and with a quick twist of the Indian's arm, forced it around in back of him. With a powerful push upward, he caused the Indian to cry out from the pain in his shoulder and elbow. The Viking then stepped behind him and with more upward force, made the Indian release the knife. While Thorvar turned momentarily to pick it up and toss it away, Wa-Gu-er'o broke the hold. He pivoted in front of Thorvar and straightened out one arm soldily against Thorvar's chest, held stiff to avoid another twist. He then grabbed his opponent with his other hand, around the back of the neck. Almost instantly, Thorvar grabbed the Indian's arm with one hand, his belt with the other and in one quick, powerful motion threw him over his head and onto the ground in back of him.

Wa-Gu-er'o rose to his feet and rushed his adversary, who was now facing him. He quickly wrapped his long arms around Thorvar's midsection, raised him up off his feet, and began squeezing him with all his strength. Thorvar dangled helplessly with no foothold, gasping for breath, and finally succeeded in getting one hand underneath the Indian's chin and the other grasping his long hair in back.

With this leverage, he began bending the taller one's head back farther and farther. Now it became a duel of strength against strength and will against will. Finally, the pain in the Indian's neck became so great from his head forced so far back that he released Thorvar, who fell limp to the ground.

With a rush, Wa-Gu-er'o ran head first at Thorvar to finish him. As he dove, intending to grab his throat and choke the remaining life out of him, Thorvar at the last instant rolled to the side. The Indian, in his desperation dive, crashed his head against a large boulder which was right behind where

Thorvar's head had been.

As the Viking started to get to his feet to avoid the next rush, he noticed that the Indian was just lying there against the boulder. When he did not move, Thorvar cautiously went over to him, alert to the possibility it might be a trick.

When there was no movement, he checked the fallen one more closely. He than rose and went over to where Nakota and Natcha were standing. He put his arm around Natcha and said quietly, "Wa-Gu-er'o is dead."

CHAPTER 25

T he three Elders came up to Thorvar, congratulated him, and one of them said, "What we have seen today will be told around our big fire for many years. We would like to know why the very tall Indian wished to kill you?"

Nakota, recognizing that his friend was out of breath, stepped in and very briefly told them of the incident in the cave of the Tall Ones.

While Thorvar was resting, Ne No took a last look around this part of the large canyon, enjoying the predominantly red and grey sides of the high canyon walls. She looked at the cliff dwellings where Natcha had played with other children. She wondered what had caused the wide black and brown streaks down the side of the cliff above this cave.

Finally, Cuerno and Kiowa called the group together and led them down along the canyon floor. By the time the sun was high in the sky, they had passed out of the entrance to the towering canyons and were heading toward the land of the setting sun, and possibly toward a big river. For Thorvar it meant the possibility of finding a way to take his family across the sea to his homeland.

After several days of travel under the hot sun, they began to realize that, as their guides had said, this was to be a tiring and rather difficult trip, and they were only getting started.

Each night they welcomed the cool darkness in this arid land. There was very little moonlight. The millions of stars were comforting, as if they were alive, not dead like so much of the land through which they were traveling.

The fourth evening, after they had eaten, Kiowa, tried to bolster their sagging spirits by telling them what he and his companion had seen on one of their earlier trips. He pointed off to the southwest and said, "Several years ago, Cuerno and I were traveling down in that direction, a distance of several days from here. We were trying to find anything we could use for a fire to cook and warm ourselves, since it was late in the year.

"We thought we saw what might be large tree trunks fallen over on their sides some distance away. This made no sense, since it was in empty land, with many sand hills ahead of us. But as we drew nearer, it seemed to be true.

We approached these large tree trunks and noticed there were no dead leaves or small branches, just tree trunks or large branches lying around.

Among the many we saw as we approached was one that lay across a deep ditch in the middle of the barren sand hills. We crossed over to the other side and noticed the end of the big, wide log was very pretty with many different colors.

"Cuerno and I got down on our knees to dig into this pretty wood. To our surprise, we could not dig into it at all, it was as hard as stone. We realized that the entire thing was rock. (Petrified Forest, near Holbrook, Arizona). All of them were solid rock. It was unbelievable, but do believe what I have told you, it is the truth."

As Thorvar and Ne No were settling down for some sleep, he leaned over and whispered to her, "Well, if I expect them to believe my truths about my homeland, I'd better believe their's." Thorvar was about to drift off to sleep when Ne No aroused him with the question, "Toe-war, if we don't like where this Kiowa is leading us, or there isn't really any river going to your great water, could we come back for a little while and live in the canyon we just left? I like it there." He turned over on his other side away from her, mumbling something she couldn't understand. She shook him by the shoulder, "Toe War! Please? Natcha liked it there, too. And we know there is water."

The Viking mumbled, "Yes. What ever you say," followed quickly by a series of disturbing snores.

The next evening, after continuing their trek across the open land, the men gathered while the women were restling.

Nakota looked over at Tanoto, "Our six men should have returned to our cliff dwellings by now. I wonder what is happening back there?"

What Natkota and Tanoto could not know was that when the six returned to their cliff dwellings, they learned that men from the various cliff dwellings had been gathering at the partly constructed temple each day since they had left. They gathered not to continue building, but to perform their ritual dances to the god, praying for the rain they needed.

They also found that some of the people had left to go about three days' travel to the southeast, to a village of stone dwellings built on the ground in the open (Aztec Ruins, New Mexico). They had heard that there was water and a very large kiva, in which a great many people could meet for ceremonial dances, including the rain dance.

The six returning travelers had dutifully told the people about their trip to the enchanting, deep canyon. They explained that Tanoto's people continuted to seek a greater supply of water for all of them.

They told of the many friendly people living there, some in cliff dwellings like theirs, others on the canyon floor by a small river. They told how crops were being grown near the river. As a result, some of the families began making preparations to go live in the canyon. Many began thinking of other places where they might go, since Tanoto and Nakota were now going too far away for them to follow.

Unaware of these plans, Tanoto's party of eight, plus Kiowa and Cuerno, resumed their trip westward the next morning. This time it was cool, since there had been an early summer rains during the night. The clouds partially blocked the sun, which gave them further relief.

They noticed the fresh smell of moisture in the air and that the countryside had taken on a thick cover of green from the temporary revival of grass and bushes. They were also able to replenish their water bags from rain water caught in bowl-like shapes in rocks and low places in the ground.

In the afternoon, as they moved wearily along, Natcha suddenly yelled out, "Look at the large half circle of many colors in the sky ahead of us! It goes into the ground on each end!" All stopped to enjoy the beautiful rainbow. The boy exclaimed, "I have seen a part of this in the mountains, but never where it went into the ground on both ends." With his eyes wide open he continued watching it until the colorful display gradually faded away.

That evening Kiowa told the group that at about high sun the next day, they would reach a river. "That river will eventually take us to the big river that flows through our very big and long canyon that I spoke of earlier."

Tanoto, expressing their graditude said, "You and Cuerno have been very valuable to us with your knowledge of the sources of drinking water and food during our trip across this land."

CHAPTER 26

T he next day when they reached the river of which Kiowa had spoken (the Little Colorado River), Thorvar was disappointed to see it was so shallow and narrow. He remembered the big river on which he and his two Viking friends had escaped in canoes from hostile Indians. Also, he remembered the even greater and wider river that they crossed before his two Viking comrades were killed by Indians the night he was captured.

He looked at Kiowa. "You call this a river. You should see the deep, wide rivers that I traveled on far back toward the rising sun. Those were rivers. This is nothing. I could not travel on this little stream in the boat I plan to build. It would never carry us to my great sea."

Kiowa smiled, "This is not the river that people from the setting sun said might go to the `big water.' This is only a small river that goes to the river in the big canyon. You will see."

They followed the river and toward early evening came to two dwellings close to the stream. When they approached, several Indians and children came running toward them. One called out, "Kiowa and Cuerno, is it you?"

The two guides ran up to their greeters, shook their hands happily and replied, "Yes, it is as you say. We have not seen you for some time."

At the dwellers' insistance they all rested near these friends of Kiowa for the night. In the morning, they gave Kiowa and Cuerno enough food to last all of them until they reached their own village. "Here is some salt for you also, Kiowa. After the long trip you told us of last night around our fire, you have need of it."

"Oh, no! You must keep it for yourselves. The food you have given us is enough."

"No, friend Kiowa. There is plenty more we can get where this river meets the greater river. You must take this salt. It will improve you and your cooking."

Kiowa laughed, "Oh, So you think I need improvement," and with that, gave him a big hug.

The friends reluctantly parted. The two guides started down along the small river as Thorvar and the group followed. Later in the morning, as they followed a curve of the river around a cliff, they saw not far ahead, a deep gorge with very high and rocky walls. It was quite a change from the flat country they had been traveling through for so many days. Because of the fairly flat ground, they were able to walk beside the river through a narrow, high walled gorge. The river was so shallow they were able to wade back and forth, looking more closely at various things on each side. As Nakota scooped up a handful of water from the stream, he said, "It's a good thing we have fresh rain water with us to drink. This water is very muddy and has a salty taste."

As Natcha started to run on ahead, Kiowa yelled sharply, "Boy, stop right where you are! Don't move! There is a big snake near you!"

Kiowa quickly grabbed a forked stick lying nearby and cautiously approached the snake from behind. With a swift thrust, he jammed the forked end of the stick behind the head of a rattlesnake. Thorvar close behind, was able to grab the snake by the tail, and with one quick motion, snapped off the reptile's head. He went over to the boy, put his arms around his shoulders and walked over to where Ne No was waiting.

When they emerged from the gorge, they climbed up on the bank to rest. None of them sat down except Kiowa and Cuerno, for before their eyes was a countryside of rippling small hills of sand as far as they could see. The desert ridges were colored in layers of grays, browns, and white. There were also larger mounds that were different shades of red! (the Painted Desert, Arizona).

The boy was the first one to speak. "This must be where the ends of those half circles of many colors in the sky touched the ground and colored these hills."

Several other shook their heads, saying, "Maybe it is the work of some of our silent gods."

They traveled beside this unusual colored earth for some time and then Kiowa led them back down by the river, which was heading into a canyon. As they continued through the canyon, the walls increased in height. After a time, they heard what sounded like the rushing of water up ahead of them.

However, it soon became too dark to travel safely in the canyon. They settled down for the night in a sandy cove, built a fire, and ate some cooked rattlesnake along with their regular food.

Thorvar, filled with anticipation as he heard the sound of water flowing nearby, had difficulty getting to sleep. At daybreak, he was up encouraging the others to rise and eat quickly so they could see what was just ahead. They hurried beside the small river until they saw the confluence of two rivers. The sound of the flowing water became louder and the walls of the canyon continued to rise in height and jaggedness.

As they came around a large rock wall, suddenly the great expanse of the canyon opened up before them. It was as if they had just walked into the depths of the earth. High above and all around them were rock walls at least three times as high as those they had seen at the canyon they had left many days ago.

The big river in front of them flowed between high canyon walls. Above the noise, Thorvar yelled to Ne No, "Now this is a river!"

They sat down on the rocks, enjoying the soothing sounds of the river, resting, and attempting to comprehend the vastness of the canyon. The walls above them were sandstone mixed with other rock and formed into many horizontal layers.

Thorvar rose and walked on down the canyon toward some large boulders with high waves spraying over them. After a short time he came running back, yelling and motioning to Kiowa and Nakota to join him. They hurried down and were amazed when the Viking showed them what he had found. It was a large, log raft, most of which was lying on the shore, lodged against the largest of the boulders. As they examined it, it was obvious to Thorvar and Kiowa that, although not recently built, it was well bound together and in good condition. The raft was partially covered with mud and weeds that had washed up on it, indicating it had not been used for some time.

The boy and Cuerno came running to see what was going on. As the men talked, Natcha spotted three long poles lying nearby. He showed them to Thorvar, who said, "These were used to guide the raft downstream, keeping it away from large rocks. This makes me think that the raft was made up river, where there are many trees. See how these logs are uneven in length and the ends have been chewed? The Indians finished the work that many beavers started. The tough vines and strips of deer hide that binds these logs together are also still in good condition."

Kiowa and Nakota agreed. They motioned to Tanoto and Nonacho to join them. "We are considering riding the raft down river to the village of Kiowa and Cuerno. They say they live in canyon not far from the river."

Tanoto replied, "But none of us has ridden on water this way. We might fall off, and some of us can't swim."

Thorvar said, "But I have ridden and guided such rafts, and I can show our men how to do it."

But the Indian persisted, "It seems to me that this river flows swiftly and we might run into places where it would be very difficult to avoid large rocks or quick drops."

"This could be. But I will keep alert to such things and if I see them ahead, we will push over to the side and quit. I will not take chances," promised Thorvar.

"Why can't we continue walking?"

Kiowa answered, "Well, to go back the way we came would take days and it would be a long walk along the upper rim of the canyon to our village. This way would be much quicker and less tiring. We cannot walk along the side of this river, because as you see ahead of us, the river flows up against the towering walls on each side."

It was decided that since five of them, Thorvar, Nakota, Natcha, Kiowa, and Cuerno, could all swim, they could look out for the three women and Tanoto. They would rest for the remainder of that day and the next to see if the people who built the raft might return for it.

When two days had passed and no one had returned to use the raft, they boarded it early in the morning and with the three poles, shoved out into the river. The water was not moving very rapidly at this point and the three men were able to control the rafts easily. The water moved faster as it passed where the river touched the walls on each side, but they used the poles against the walls and avoided any problems.

After a while, they came to a wider part of the river in a more open space in the canyon. They floated on down the river for some time when Thorvar and Kiowa heard a roaring sound farther ahead. As they floated along the roaring grew louder. Thorvar became concerned about the possibility of rapids or maybe a water fall. He directed them to use their poles, pushing against rocks in the water to guide them to the sandy shore. Tanoto was pushing so hard on the poles that he suddenly lost his balance when the lower end of the pole slipped off a rock under the water. He fell head first into the river. When he surfaced, he frantically grabbed a small log floating by, and held on for dear life.

The current quickly carried him down stream toward the roar of water. Thorvar hesitated for an instant, torn between his responsibility to those on the raft and to Tanoto. After this delay of valuable seconds, he dove into the river and started swimming with powerful strokes after Tanoto. The delay and the increasing swiftness of the river became a real challenge to the Viking.

He continued to close the gap between them as they got closer to the roar, which Thorvar now realized was from a water fall. When he was only several hundred feet from the top of the falls, he grabbed frantically at the branches of the small log, got a hold of it, and yelled to Tanoto, "Keep hold on to this log! Flatten out and start kicking your legs up and down fast!!" Thorvar used his free arm to stroke, his powerful legs to kick and with Tanoto's kicking they began to move toward shore.

Finally, after a supreme effort, the Viking managed to get them behind some large boulders. He was then able to plant his feet on the river bottom, away from the current. They rested there recovering their breath and strength Tanoto still holding tightly onto the small log. Thorvar then carried Tanoto, who was physically and emotionally exhausted, on to the riverbank.

After resting for some time, they were joined by Nakota and Kiowa, who obviously were overjoyed to find them both alive. They walked down the river to look at the waterfall. It was a long fall into some very wild rapids.

When Ne No and Tanoto's mate saw that they had landed safely, they ran toward them with outstretched arms. Ne No cupped her hands around her man's neck, placed her head against his chest and sighed, "I thought I had really lost you this time."

CHAPTER 27

T he area where they landed their raft was an open part of the canyon. They could see hills and ledges of rock between the river and the distant walls. The group contemplated their next move. They could not go back up river because of the section where the water flowed up against the sheer canyon walls. They might go downstream by climbing up and over some high hills around the falls and rapids, but they had no way of knowing whether they might become trapped by more high walls and narrow passages, with no place to climb out.

The men decided to look for ways to climb out of the canyon, since there seemed to be no alternative. They spread out in pairs, Natcha with Thorvar, Nakota with Nonacho, and Kiowas with Cuerno. Tanoto stayed with the women for their protection and to rest from his harrowing experience.

It was understood that since it was late in the morning, and darkness would settle in earlier because of the depth of the canyon, that only a brief exploratory search should be made that day. Late in the afternoon, two groups returned without any good news. Just as darkness was about to descend upon the canyon, Kiowa and Cuerno quietly returned with some good news.

They had found a trail which they had followed upward for a time. "Sorry we are late getting back but Cuerno and I had to see if this trail might lead where we want it to go. We think it may."

The next morning they started up the path, somewhat subdued, realizing that if it did go up to the rim of the canyon, it would be a long, hot, and difficult climb. By early afternoon they had climbed about one third of the way up the sloping canyon, following the trail back and forth as it wound its way gradually upward. They stopped to rest frequently. The trail ended abruptly at the bottom of a cliff. Slowly making their way around it, they climbed over piles of rocks of various sizes and shapes that had fallen from the cliff and lodged around its base. As they came around one high pile of rocks, they were surprised to see a relatively flat terrace spread out before them. They also saw three small rock dwellings nestled on the ground at the base of the cliff.

As they approached, many adults and a number of children came to greet them. They noticed crops growing in a fairly level area beside their dwellings and a spring nearby.

One of the older men stepped forward, bowed to Tanoto and said, "You are welcome. We know you are not enemies because you have women with you."

Tanoto replied, "It is so. We only seek to get to the top to continue our journey. Can you tell us how we should go."

"It would be difficult to tell you. I will guide you all to the top, but now it is too late in the day. Rest with us and tomorrow I will show you the way."

"We don't want to bother you and your people," replied Tanoto.

"It is no bother. We would like you to visit with us. Living here, we see few other people."

They spent the rest of that day resting. In the evening they gathered around the fire, talking about each other's lives. Tanoto and his people were interested to learn that the people lived in the lower part of the canyon because there was a longer growing season than there was on the rim. More foods were available in the canyon, such as mountain sheep, rabbits, berries, and fruit from cactus plants. Water was available from many springs as well as from the river. They were also more protected from the winter storms.

By noon the next day, their friendly guide had brought them to the top. From there, while resting on the rim of this canyon, they were able to see the immense size and the awe inspiring depth and beauty of the canyon. (The Grand Canyon)

As Thorvar looked in amazement down into the depths of the vast canyon, with all its rock formations, he exclaimed, "It looks like a great mountain that has sunk into a tremendous hole. See all the peaks and separate valley, and the white ribbon of the river flowing below."

Ne No replied, "Yes, and look at all the different colors and shapes in those great mountainous rocks."

For the next few days they followed the rim of the canyon, stopping often to enjoy its grandeur and its changing beauty at different times of the day. They often saw rock dwellings built along the rim, and briefly visited with some of the people.

They left the rim of the canyon as it veered to the right, and continued straight ahead across open country.

When they stopped to rest Kiowa said, "We are heading for a smaller canyon that will take us back down into the bigger canyon we have just left. It will take us to our village, where my people live."

CHAPTER 28

L ate in the day, as they moved along, Kiowa pointed in the direction they were going. "Up on that hilltop among the small, bushy trees is where we will spend the night before starting down."

Nakota shielded his eyes from the setting sun and said, "Wasn't that a deer I just saw running among those trees?"

"Yes. You may have occasionaly noticed deer among the trees during the past few days. We depend on deer for food during the dry seasons."

Thorvar, anticipating their arrival at Kiowa's village and the river that might take them to the sea, said, "Which way do we go in the morning toward your village?"

Kiowa noticed Thorvar's veiled excitement, smiled, and pointed off to the right. "We start down into the canyon right over there."

"How soon will we arrive at your village?"

"When the sun is high. It will take some time going down through this smaller canyon."

"Are there trees down there?"

"Yes."

"And lots of water?"

"Yes."

Thorvar grabbed Ne No's hand and motioned to Natcha and Nakota to follow. They walked over to the head of the canyon and looked down. It was very steep.

Nakota said, "We'd better get back and get some rest. It looks from here as if it will be a rough trip down tomorrow."

True to Nakota's prediction, the trip to the canyon floor, a thousand feet below, was difficult. The trail was a series switchbacks, which required caution and slow progress. Finally, they reached the canyon floor. The trail then crossed a dry wash and went between two very high sandstone cliffs.

As they passed between the cliffs, the boy yelled to Thorvar, "Look! It is so narrow here that I can almost touch both walls at the same time." When he noticed an echo from the words he had just yelled he called out, "Ne No! Listen to the echoes bouncing from the walls above us!" Then he yelled again.

But Ne No and the rest of them were looking in amazement at the clearing they had just entered. "Toe-war! Look at all the big green trees. Look at the greenness all around!"

"And look at the spring just ahead flowing into the stream," sighed

Tanoto. "I've never seen such a beautiful, green valley like this before."

All of the adults just stood and enjoyed looking at this lovely valley. But not Natcha. In his boyish glee, he raced ahead and into the stream where it widened out. As he splashed around in it, he yelled, "It feels so good on my feet and legs!"

The others began wading across the stream. Half way across, they all stopped to cool their feet. Soon the three women began splashing each other. Kiowa, Cuerno and Tanoto lay down in the cool water.

Tanoto said quietly, "I may just lie here the rest of the day."

Nonacho grabbed his sister and threw her into the water.

Thorvar just stood back, grinning. "Now maybe you can see why I love the rivers and the sea so much. They bring life and beauty and adventure."

Finally, Kiowa induced them to continue on the path. As they proceeded happily, dripping water, he said, "Wait 'til you see what's beyond the rise ahead."

They hurried forward and, as they topped the hill, they saw another beautiful, green, narrow valley with many trees, surrounded by high red rock formations, eight hundred feet high.

This time the Viking was impressed. "This reminds me of several places back in my country, with all the greenness and big trees and the protection of the high cliffs. And look at the tall rock formations, that one there looks like a small castle standing out from the sheer wall."

Kiowa, encouraged by their enthusiasm, called out, "Yes, and our dwellings are over by the big trees. This is where we live all year." (Village of Supia).

Thorvar went over and put his arm around Kiowa's shoulder, and said, "But, my friend, where is the large river that may go to the sea?"

"Do not be concerned, big man. We are not yet down into the lowest part of the canyon where your river flows. I will take you down the trail tomorrow. But today, we must stay among our people and get you settled."

"Yes. This is true. But tomorrow I must see that river!"

As they approached the dwellings, curious people began gathering under many of the large, shady trees. Some of the children ran to greet Kiowa and Cuerno, holding their arms up to be lifted.

Ne No was pleased to see that the childrens' heads were round, not flat in the back like those of many of their cliff children. As she came nearer, she also noticed that the people, like the children, did not have this flatness in back. She thought it gave them a thinner, nicer looking face like Toe-war's. She was glad that her father had not permitted her mother to flatten the back of her head.

She later conveyed these thoughts to Thorvar, and added, "However, they don't look to be as strong and broad in the shoulders as our men." Thorvar remarked, "It may be because they haven't had to walk distances and climb cliffs, carrying large rocks to build their dwellings. They have wood and rocks and water close by. Even their crops are planted right here in the valley, and are easily watered. It reminds me of my home in some ways."

Kiowa's people built a large fire that evening to welcome the newcomers. They also fed them. They were a friendly, happy people, who, earlier in the afternoon, had learned much from Kiowa and Cuerno about their guests. So that evening they didn't ask questions of these people, although they were curious, especially about the big pale-face man and the tall Indian boy. They enjoyed entertaining the newcomers with several of their tribal dances and chants.

The next morning, while Tanoto, Nonacho, Cuerno, and several of his friends were building temporary shelters for the visitors, Thorvar and Nakota followed Kiowa toward the large river the Viking was so anxious to see.

Thorvar caught up to Kiowa and said, "During the night I thought I heard a roaring sound not too far away, like water falling. Was it the big river?"

"No. It is still some distance from here, down below. What you heard was a waterfall just a short distance ahead. We will soon be there."

The roar grew louder as they followed a trail around a projecting cliff and suddenly saw a beautiful waterfall plunging into the depths (Navajo Falls).

Thorvar stopped to admire it saying, "This also reminds me of my home, the mist in my face, the roaring sound. But the color of the water? It changes from pale blue to blue-green as it falls. This is different."

Thorvar was about to sit on a rock to enjoy this soothing feeling he had missed so much, but Kiowa said, "We have much walking and climbing to do. We must go. This is nearby. You can visit it later."

Nakota was already moving ahead. They joined him, with Kiowa taking the lead. They followed the trial that descended and then climbed again to land above. Kiowa turned back toward them. "We will stay close to the side of the cliff just ahead and then climb to a place where there is a view of another waterfall (Havasu Falls). It falls even farther."

After arriving and viewing it from above, Thorvar hurried down to its base. As he approached the circular pool directly below the falls, he saw three children splashing around in it. One of them was Natcha.

When Thorvar approached the edge, Natcha spotted him and yelled above the roar of the falls, "Hi Thorvar! Isn't this great? I love it here!" Thorvar cupped his hands around his mouth and shouted, "Yes! I do too! How's the water?" As the boy received a splash in the face, he yelled, "It's just right, not too hot, not too cold!"

The Viking looked from the pool on up the cliff and saw, high above, a separated stream of water tumbling out of a cave-like hole in the cliff, falling into the round pool of blue-green water where the children were swimming.

By this time Kiowa and Nakota had joined him. "My friend, Nakota, look at the beauty here, the blue pool and the banks covered with moss."

Nakota nodded his head, "Yes, I see it. But I'd rather be down in that water with the young ones. Let's move along and get this trip to `your' river over with so I can do such things."

Kiowa let out a happy laugh and said, "Come on you two, you have a long ways to go yet and there is more to see. We'll leave this waterfall for your son to enjoy. He'll be all right, he's with two of my sons."

They followed the stream a fairly short distance until they approached a third waterfall (Mooney Falls). They reached the top and looked down into the valley far below. Thorvar was trilled by this great falls, which was the highest of the three.

He looked over at Kiowa and asked, "How do we get down there from here? This is a sheer, wide cliff with no way down that I can see."

"There is a way, but it is slow and hard to climb. Instead, we will climb down through some caves and passageways that lead to the bottom of the falls."

They climbed through caves and around boulders until they emerged into the valley below. It was very green. There was cactus, many large cottonwood trees, and a beautiful pool with rock shelves back under the falls.

Thorvar saw this and started to go underneath, behind the wall of falling water. Kiowa called to him, "We'll do that on our return trip. We still have a long way to go if you want to get to your river and back today!"

They resumed walking and climbing down through the canyon, following the stream. When the sun was high overhead they reached the bottom. There Thorvar saw the river flowing swiftly by. They walked out onto a small, sandy beach where the clear, blue-green water of the stream flowed into the muddy water of the river.

They sat down to rest and look up at the high canyon walls above them, all except Thorvar. His full attention was now on the river and the possibility of getting to the sea.

He walked along the bank for some distance, climbing up on large boulders and high places so he could see as far as possible. He returned to where his companions were sitting on the sand, cooling their feet in the clear stream. Kiowa and Nakota were talking about the amount of water and way of life in this canyon country, so different from where Nakota and his people lived.

The Viking sat down but said nothing. After a long silence he quietly said, "Well, I may be able to do something, but it won't be easy. I could see some rough water up ahead, enough that I don't think I could use a raft, such as we used farther back on the river."

Nakota came over and sat down beside him. "My friend, I will be sad if you leave us. Do not worry, we will help you find a way."

Thorvar put his hand on his friend's knee, "Yes, We will find a way, my Nakota. I would not ask you to leave your people. But you are welcome to go with us."

Kiowa looked over at the two of them. "I have heard that where this river finally flows out of the canyon it becomes very smooth. But the land at that point has no trees to make a raft."

The three of them stretched out on the beach, resting before they started their long climb back up to Kiowa's village. They watched birds, high above, flying between the canyon walls. They saw fish break the surface of the water, capturing insects and other bits of food. They lay in the sunshine, apparently contented. But Thorvar was troubled. He felt disappointed, but could not give up. Suddenly he jumped up, waved his arms high over his head and cried. "I've got it, I know what I will do!"

Both of the others sat up, looking at him inquiringly. "I was thinking about the time my two Norse friends and I were captured by Indians, and we escaped in a canoe they had made. It was so light that when we ran into rough water, we just picked it up and carried it along the shore until the rough water was behind us. Then we put the canoe back in the river and continued. I will make a canoe big enough for Ne No, Natcha, and myself. The boy is big enough that he can help me carry the canoe around any rough water."

"But, how will you make a canoe and from what?" Nakota asked.

"The three of us, while in captivity, watched the Indians make a canoe. I think I can do it. Also at the settlement by the sea, I watched some friendly Indians make a boat something like a canoe, by burning out the long center part of a large log laid sideways. They shaped the outside, the bow, and the stern using stone axes. A boat like this would be much heavier to carry. But if I can't build one of them, I can try to build the other."

Nakota and Kiowa looked questioningly at each other, but Thorvar, now in high spirits, said, "I'm ready to go back up to your village." He looked at Kiowa. "Don't you think we should go now?"

Kiowa led the way. They climbed, rested, and climbed some more. They finally reached the base of the highest falls. Thorvar went back under the wall of falling water to sit and enjoy the cooling mist on his face and arms. He was joined by the other two, who cooled off in the pool at that base of the falls.

After this refreshing rest, they resumed their way back up through the caves and passed by the other two falls. When they returned to the village, Thorvar turned to Kiowa and said, "You and your people have a grand place to live."

That evening, Thorvar took Ne No by the hand and they walked down to the first waterfall. They sat on some large rocks while Thorvar thought about telling her what he had seen that day, and of his plans. But after they had been there only a short time, Ne No started slapping at the mosquitoes buzzing around her head. She jumped up and said in no uncertain terms, "Toe-war, let's go back up to the village and sit by the big fire. I do want to see all those grand waterfalls you saw today. Let's do it tomorrow during the day, when those pesky things aren't around."

CHAPTER 29

ater that evening he told her of the difficulties he anticipated if they continued their trip to the sea. He reviewed with her his plans for building a boat in which they could continue their trip down the river, through the bigger canyon, and beyond.

When Ne No seemed disinterested, Thorvar lifted her chin with his hand, looked into her lovely eyes, and said, "Ne No, you don't seem to be interested in continuing this trip."

She bowed her head and quietly said, "Where you go, I go."

The next morning Ne No awoke early and shook Thorvar. "Toe-war, wake up! I want you to show me those waterfalls now."

Thorvar and Ne No walked down the path toward the first waterfall. The grass and bushes were glistening with the dew of the early morning. They heard birds all around them singing their early morning songs. The air was fresh with the clean smell of the valley, surrounded by the high, red-rocked walls that framed it.

They followed the trail around the cliff and sat down beside the waterfall where Ne No had spent a few uncomfortable moments the night before.

"I did not know that water could be so blue," she exclaimed, as they watched the water falling from the precipice. "This is lovely."

"Yes, but wait 'til I show you the other two falls."

And with that, he grabbed her hand and moved on down the trail.

She stopped suddenly and said, "Wait! I want to look at these large white flowers with their blossoms open up so wide. Aren't they pretty? We had some pretty flowers back near our cliffs, but not like these."

They went farther on and then climbed a short hill. He held her hand tightly as they eased along the path where it narrowed up against the cliff, and then came into the clear when they could see the next waterfall.

She broke loose and hurried on ahead. As he caught up with her, her mouth half open and her eyes wide, she turned to him and said, "Isn't this beautiful? Look how the blue water divides and falls from that wide ledge, as if there were two or three separate falls. And look at the light colored rock (travertine) attached hanging down from where the water starts to fall."

"Yes, Ne No. I see it. See all the pink and gray and orange colors in the rock of the cliff. This is where I found Natcha swimming in the pool below with two of Kiowa's boys."

He showed her the third falls, where the water leaped into the valley far below.

Ne No exclaimed, "Isn't this beautiful, Toe-war? I love it here. Do you?"

"Yes. It reminds me of parts of my homeland."

That night Torvar lay awake for a long time, thinking about how much Ne No seemed to be enjoying this valley. He said to himself, "I have never seen her so happy and full of life. And the boy, in this short time, has already made several friends. The people are so friendly. The water and the crops seemed to be so abundant."

He began weighing these things against his burning desire to get back to his homeland and his own people. He also thought about reaching the sea, and even more unlikely, about the possibility of finding a ship there.

The next morning, Tanoto and Nonacho told Thorvar that they and their mates wished to stay in this valley because it was so fertile and pleasant. "We wondered if you might ask Kiowa, who seems to be very friendly toward you, if we might stay and live here among these people? It is too far to return this year to our cliff dwellings especially since our two mates are 'with child'."

Thorvar saw Kiowa passing nearby and he and Tanoto approached him, "Kiowa, Tanoto and Nonacho would like to know if they and their mates can remain here and live among your people?"

Kiowa smiled and replied,"I think so. But let me ask our Elders."

Tanoto interrupted, "We are not sure your people want those from another tribe to live near them."

"Well, I don't think that would be of concern. Our people are of what we now call the Pai tribe, which includes former members of the Walapai and Havasupai tribes."

Later that afternoon, three Elders approached Tanoto's people and said, "We will give you seed to plant your crops. You are welcome."

Tanoto, Nonacho, and their mates thanked them and immediately began planning where they would build their dwellings.

Later, Nakota called Tanoto and Nonacho aside and said, "Shouldn't I return to our cliff dwellings and tell our people of this place, where there is plenty of water? This is why we came on this trip."

Tanoto replied, "No, It is not necessary. Our mission was to go to the land of the three joined canyons farther back and tell our people of the amount of water there. This had been done."

"But if Thorvar does not need me, I could go back and and tell them of this place. I could show them the way when I return."

Tanoto placed his hands on Nakota's shoulders, "Do not be concerned, my loyal friend. It would be a hard trip for you to make following the one we have just completed. But more than that, it would be too long a journey for so many of our people to make. Be content and enjoy this new land with us." Then he poked him in the side, and, looking out of the corner of his eyes said, "You might even find a mate among these friendly people. Remember, this winter the nights may be a little cool."

When the people learned that Tanoto, Nonacho, their mates, and Nakota were going to stay and live among them, many came to the big fire that evening to welcome them.

Kiowa found Thorvar and Ne No sitting off to one side. "There you are, my friend. Why don't you two and your son stay and live with us? You would be most welcome."

Thorvar shook his head. "If we did, I don't know what I'd do. I need to move around."

Kiowa laughed loudly and said, "That is no problem. Not too far from here, beyond the other side of the big canyon where the river flows, is a land of many great stone arches (Arches National Monument, Utah); also many tall rocks of pink, red and white which you and Nakota can go to with Cuerno and me (Bryce Canyon, Utah). And, oh yes, not too far from there is a place with a quiet stream that wanders among tall shade trees" (Zion National Park, Utah).

The Norseman spent another restless night tossing and turning. Finally, Ne No sat up on their mat and said, "Toe-War. What is troubling you?"

He rolled over, looked up at her and quietly asked, "Ne No, would you like to live here for maybe a year among your people? You would rest from our recent long trip while I decide whether we should try to return to my homeland."

She snuggled down beside him, and with a little chuckle of happiness, softly replied, "Yes, I think maybe we should." Then there was a pause before she whispered, "Especially since I am 'with child' again."

As he hugged her joyfully in his massive arms, she stuck her head out and giggled, "Living in this happy place, we three women from the cliff dwellings just might be starting a whole new tribe in this beautiful valley."

AUTHOR'S COMMENTS:

So Ne No and Thorvar and their group, did stay in this beautiful valley that winter, and the people in Mesa Verde were told of the water available in Canyon de Chelly.

It is interesting to note that in a recent publication of the Southwestern Parks and Monuments Association, the following comments appeared concerning Canyon de Chelly.

"The seven rooms built on the central ledge, including a three story tower, were constructed (near Mummy Cave) and are identified as being of *Mesa Verde type masonry*. Tree rings dating techniques indicate that the tower was built about AD 1284."

"Archeologists believe that the architects were people who had left Mesa Verde area in southwestern Colorado, perhaps after being pushed out of their homeland by drought and other conditions of stress."

Hmmmmm. VERY INTERESTING.

A. Tanner Smith